LAND LUST
JOGINDER PAUL

LAND LUST
JOGINDER PAUL

Short Stories

Translated from the original Urdu

Editors

Sukrita Paul Kumar
Vandana R Singh

NIYOGI
BOOKS

Published by
NIYOGI BOOKS
Block D, Building No. 77,
Okhla Industrial Area, Phase-I,
New Delhi-110 020, INDIA
Tel: 91-11-26816301, 26818960
Email: niyogibooks@gmail.com
Website: www.niyogibooksindia.com

Inhouse Editor: Vibha Kumar
Design: Shashi Bhushan Prasad/Cover: Misha Oberoi

ISBN: 978-93-86906-80-9
Publication: 2019

Printed at: Niyogi Offset Pvt. Ltd., New Delhi, India

Contents

Preface *by Editors*   7

Foreword *by Krishan Chander*   11
Translated by Punya Prakash Tripathi

STORIES

Miracle   17
Translated by Keerti Ramachandra

Seeking Answers   29
Translated by Keerti Ramachandra

The Slump   37
Translated by Chandana Dutta

When Life Dies   45
Translated by Vandana R Singh

Land Lust   55
Translated by Keerti Ramachandra

Jambo Rafiqui   65
Translated by Usha Nagpal

Multiracial   81
Translated by Meenakshi Bharat

0   87
Translated by Chandana Dutta

Rascal   99
Translated by Meenakshi Bharat

Everywhere   109
Translated by Meenakshi Bharat

Cast in the Same Mould   123
Translated by Usha Nagpal

Jambo, Joginder Paul!   134
Translated by Chandana Dutta

Glossary   138

Other Works *by Joginder Paul*   140

Acknowledgements   144

Preface

S oon after the Partition of the country and just after getting out of the refugee camp in 1948 at Ambala, when Joginder Paul was a young twenty three-year-old writer, he married a girl from Kenya on the condition that they would settle in Kenya. A refugee that he was anyway, he migrated with her to a country which was still in the clutches of the British rule while, ironically, his own country India had just won its hard-earned freedom. Pained by the social inequality and racial discrimination that he witnessed in everyday life there, he felt like a complete outsider. The Asian community around him seemed to accept that social reality as a given and, in fact, participated fully in its perpetuation. He considered himself 'in exile', and longed to get back to his homeland from the day he landed there.

The stories in this volume emerged from his anguish and sensitive observation of the lives of Asians living in Kenya, especially in their relationship/non- relationship with Africans. Originally called *Dharti ka Kaal, Land Lust* is a collection of eleven stories that capture the spirit and social ambience of Indians living in pre-independence, colonised Kenya. The presence of African characters in these stories, in a way, asserts the dignity of the black people otherwise invisible in urban social domain there.

The Kenya of 1950s was a multiracial society where the British, Asians, and Africans co-existed in a harshly xenophobic environment. The lure of money, 'development project' of African cities, the beautiful weather and the 'highlands' drew people from all over to Kenya. The stories in this volume unravel the sensitivity of the author to the incipient racism and the operative colonial hierarchies, as also the tussle between nature and 'development'.

Jambo Rafiqui, one of Paul's most brilliant stories in this book, deftly explores the naivety of the locals while also giving us a glimpse of the social pecking order, complicated as it is by the presence of Asians who hang in an uneasy balance between the black and the white. Here and elsewhere too what quietly emerges is the belief in the superiority of one's own race that runs uniformly across the spectrum – it's a different matter that only the colonisers overtly declare themselves to be so.

The dynamics between different races and cultural groups takes on thought-provoking overtones when we see Indians having absolutely no doubt about their own superior culture, and ruing over the fact that there is no 'life' in Kenya and no intelligent people to have a decent conversation with. This coming from people with a two hundred-year-long history of being colonised themselves gives a glimpse of a knotted world where the oppressed waste no time in reinventing themselves as oppressors. Most Indian characters seem to suffer from complete amnesia regarding the recent Partition of their own country – a haphazard decision perpetrated by the very same imperialists with whom they tend to mindlessly align themselves in another colonised landscape. And so, we are face-to-face with a tangled, convoluted world where racism doesn't come only in shades of white and black but is a knotted web with liberal sprinkling of brown. Interestingly, and sadly, most of these themes are still alive today. The context of the stories is historical but the themes are as relevant today as then.

While in one of the stories young African boys are asked to dive into a killer lake for a coin by an Asian family, in another story, Jaroge – an enthusiastic and well-meaning African employee – becomes a victim of institutional racism when he is abruptly fired from his job.

Joginder Paul's fiction does not ignore any of the harsh aspects of the social reality in Kenya then – be it racism by the British government, in educational institutions, by farm owners, businessmen, or staid homemakers. Paul can see through it all, and create a world around these themes for the readers to get a peek at the bleak, deeper reality under the superficial cheer of a large class of people in Kenya in mid-twentieth century. Irrespective of where one was situated in the social ladder or positioned in a given power structure, most people seem to be content with the state of affairs.

Through these stories, Joginder Paul's keen eye and artful storytelling brings alive an empathy for fellow human beings, evoking the reader's capability to see beyond opaque exteriors. This is something as desirable today as earlier when the stories were written. The social follies, political foibles, and oppressive power structures continue to exist and percolate into everyday lives of ordinary people. While the stories in *Land Lust* offer a poignant slice of colonial history of lives led in the pre-independence multiracial Kenya, we believe they bring to the fore themes of universal appeal across cultures and time.

Sukrita Paul Kumar
Vandana R Singh

Foreword

Krishan Chander

When I first met Joginder Paul, his demeanour, his manner and personality led me to think that he was a wealthy connoisseur of jewels. Soon, I realized I was not very much off the mark. A connoisseur indeed, but not of gold and silver. He is a connoisseur of stories; he is prosperous, but only in his art.

Joginder Paul has ushered a new ethos into the world of Urdu short stories. Africa is not merely a land of green parrots and long-necked giraffes. A lot of people tell tales about a kind of Africa that is barbaric. Joginder Paul talks of people who are referred to not just as Africans but as habshis. All sorts of ugly stories about their character and personality have been instilled into our consciousness. Not only does Joginder Paul demolish incorrect tales by introducing new characters in the new environs, he also tells us very interesting things about the social reality of colonial Kenya and its people. He is the first Urdu writer to have walked us through the many facets of African lives with such finesse and expertise.

Paul has his own distinct point of view. Most people don't have any specific way of looking at things. They stop and see, entertain themselves and walk away. Indeed, that in itself can also be seen as representative of a point of view, but an extremely superficial one. Joginder Paul too stops and looks; he too entertains and walks away but even after his going away, we keep relishing his short stories because the scene he presents to us is not superficial like in many other cases. His stories present several layers of meaning which he slowly unfolds and seems to find joy in doing so again and again. What peeps from his stories is the heart of an empathetic writer, someone who is pro-humanity. He is not merely like the plate in a camera on which the surface surroundings are imprinted, he possesses an empathetic perspective too. He has the space in his heart for the other's pain and anguish. Inside many other writers is placed merely a camera and in place of a heart, there is a typewriter.

Joginder Paul is fortunate that he is not one of those writers. He has a distinct, humane point of view that looks to the betterment and welfare of people. Moreover, he is fully conscious of the responsibility of his pen.

Paul is a young writer who belongs to the new generation. I am not really concerned about who belongs to the new or the old generation; I am only bothered by who writes well and who doesn't, who is a good writer and who isn't. Some people may start writing well at the young age of twenty while others are destined to acquire the fine art of writing much later, sometimes only after crossing the age of fifty. Different kinds of examples are found in literature. In order to assess someone's writing, age is certainly not a criterion to be bothered about. What needs to be discerned is whether the writing measures up to being good literature.

As an admirer of English literature, Joginder Paul has learnt a lot from Western literature in relation to his own writing, like all of us have. But in as far as his point of view is concerned, it is in no way 'Western'. In general, artists don't seem to be engaging with the living and changing realities of the East, in the same way as others tend to ignore the larger realities of the world. Much against their wishes, perhaps, the major focus of the world today seems to be shifting from art to science, and then from science to politics. Perhaps the writer is unable to first face and then accept this phenomenon. That is why they tend to become inward and remain busy with their internal life.

Not so in the case of Joginder Paul. He cannot be accused of being dismissive of the social and political realities of the world outside of himself. He could very easily have suppressed his awareness and anxieties about his immediate surroundings; he could have ignored deeper realities and remained at the surface level by depicting the colours and shapes of superficial reality through his fine art. But he did not do this, and in not doing this, he worked with great courage. Paul's context is that of East Africa. The people of East Africa are like the Pathans of the subcontinent – straightforward and simple. They have a rather uncomplicated sensibility. Here if Nature is elemental, the human being too is like a child, innocent and trusting. Some people who went there from the West have created settlements there. They have built railways and mines, cleared forests, cultivated farms in the valleys and while doing this, they have – like in the other parts of Africa – made East Africans dependent on themselves. In this way, neither does the land or the country belong to Africans, nor is the rule theirs. While they are in their own country, they have become servants of people from outside. There are some Hindustani people amongst them too who – though on a smaller scale – also exploit the Africans. These are some basic facts regarding life in East Africa today which, if ignored, would mean dismissing very important realities of life there.

Joginder Paul could have entertained himself by simply presenting what he witnessed as the lives of the rich and the glamorous world of the outsiders. Those would have been fun stories through which the self-centred reality of those people could have been revealed. While the joy of reading the stories is retained by the writer, thanks to his exposure to Western literature, he also weaves a creative intrigue in his stories. He knows very well how to give a bit of a jerk or a surprise at the end of the story. There is not a single sentence more than necessary in his writing and, unlike some older writers like myself, he does not lean on surfeit of words. He comes across as very knowledgeable about the art of writing a short story and, within this form, he does not need to learn from anyone. By remaining truthful to his art, he has, in fact, chosen to be on a very difficult path. His sympathies are not with the profiteering foreigners, nor is he biased or aligned with the people from his own country. His empathy is with the poor native Africans who actually belong to that country and are determined to fight for their freedom.

What kind of people are they? What kind of lives do they lead? How do they love? What kind of land do they live on? What is its shape and colour? What has the so-called new civilization brought into their old jungles? Don't listen to the wondrous tales about all these matters from me. Listen to them from Joginder Paul who has narrated them beautifully, artfully, and aesthetically through this collection of short stories in a way that life in Africa comes alive and flashes with its varied colours in the eyes of the reader.

Translated by Punya Prakash Tripathi

*This article was written in 1959 by eminent Urdu writer Krishan Chander

Miracle

•

Mojaza

When I pulled over close to a rough path on the left side of the main road, a bunch of grubby African children gathered around our car.

'From here on, you will have to walk to the lake, sir,' one of the boys came up to me and said.

All of us got out of the car muttering. We unloaded the picnic material, locked the now empty car and started discussing how we were going to walk to the spot. Without waiting to be told, two African boys picked up all our stuff – as if believing that it was their job to carry our burden. The other kids, rubbing their noses on their sleeves or scratching their heads, looked at the lucky ones enviously as they stood before us, cheerfully bearing our load.

'Keep an eye on them ji,' my wife said eyeing them suspiciously, as she proceeded to straighten the muffler around Harish's neck.

Little Titu became restless, wanting to be carried. Seizing the opportunity, one of the African boys stepped forward and picked Titu up fondly in his arms. Pleased with himself, he went and stood alongside his companions, who carried our burden with great pride, thinking that if they could earn a shilling or two that day, their parents would be very pleased with them and would even embrace them fondly. Finally, our little procession set off on the mile-and-a-half-long trek along the muddy path to the shores of the lake below. My wife looked at me again, as if to say 'be careful of these black urchins'. 'These fellows are very crooked, if you are not alert, they'll hoodwink you and run off with all our stuff,' she announced.

'Ma ji, just see the magical power of the Creator.' My wife always speaks to Ma ji in her own language and tone. 'This is a lake, isn't it? On top is the earth while down below there's water and, more water,' she had told her this many times before, 'and when you walk on it, this is how the earth moves under your feet!' Raising her right hand high, she said, 'Watch the Creator's magical power.' And Ma ji, in her usual style, replied, 'Sat Naam Shri Wahe Guru.'

My six-year-old son Suresh was asking an African boy, 'What class are you studying in?' The African boy didn't reply, but gave a faint smile, perhaps wondering if he did go to school what class he would be in.

Perhaps his father's simple, straightforward answer echoed in his ears: 'What do we want with education, son? Mungu has created us to do work. Reading and writing is for the idle. Go get on with your work.' The African boy seemingly stopped for a moment, as if to say to his father petulantly 'that's what I am doing, Baba, working!'

***

He was carrying our fruit basket in his left hand and the tiffin carrier in his right. Suddenly, a ripe red apple rolled out of the basket. 'Be careful, you idiot!' My wife's flashing gaze rested on the toppling apple.

Rita quickly grabbed the apple and sank her sharp teeth into it. 'It's really sweet, Mummy,' she said.

Seeing the apple safe in the girl's mouth, my wife turned her attention to Ma ji again. 'Ma ji, the price of apples is soaring very high this year. These very apples I used to buy for one shilling. Now, no one lets you even touch them for less than three.'

'Mummy, do apples grow like pumpkins along the ground or like mangoes on a tree?' asked Rita.

'Where I live,' the African boy started saying to Harish, 'there are countless number of trees with huge apples.'

'Really?'

'Yes. Even if you keep eating them all your life, they won't finish.' The African boy seemed to be wondering what apples tasted like. 'Wazungu puts them into sacks and sends them to the city.'

'You people must be eating lots of apples?'

'No. We eat boiled maize flour. My Baba says it is very tasty.'

'Sat Naam Shri Wahe Guru!'

We turned left onto a narrow track to get to the lake where, instead of human beings, we could see rows of tiny insects crawling along. On this dark subcontinent, on deserted paths, different kinds of creatures get trampled upon by strangers. And they give up their lives without a scream.

Four or five years ago, a dangerous group of black terrorists had created a big turmoil in these parts, just the way insects start swarming about in agitation when they are disturbed. But for how long? Today, there is a death-like silence here, which seems all the more dense because of the guffaws of some strangers who are picnicking.

Suddenly, I was bitten on the ankle by an insect. Hopping about in pain, I glared at it, crushed it ruthlessly under my foot and threw it away.

'Ma ji, at one time this region was very dangerous,' my wife explained to Ma ji. 'Some black goons had their stronghold here, they were self-appointed colonels and generals, and had become quite tyrannical. Thank God the government rounded up each one of them, or we would have been in trouble... We would have had to abandon our running businesses and leave.'

'Mummy,' Suresh chipped in with bravado, 'when I grow up I'm also going to be a general, and with my pistol I will shoot like this.' Turning his hands into a pistol, he pointed to one of the African lads and shouted, 'Boom...boom!'

'Sure Beta, shabash. Ma ji, these people ask for independence, but someone should ask these barbarians what they will do with that freedom. Let them get an education first. After all, running a country is not child's play.'

'What you say is true, *beti*. British rule is indeed the best.'

'We also struggled hard for our country's freedom,' said my wife, as if convincing herself, but then our case was different. 'Where's the comparison between us and these savages? Just think Ma ji, our culture is so old, so ancient, and our religion is several thousand years older than even the religion of the British. These people have learnt to make bombs only now but the *Ramayana* says that just one arrow from Shri Rama's bow could destroy the whole world.'

'Sat Naam Sri Wahe Guru! You are right, *beti*. Our religion is great. It's because of our good deeds that one is born a Hindu. That's why I don't let my *boi* step into the kitchen. Who knows what kind of half-cooked or raw meat these people eat.'

Just then we saw a stark naked African youth bounding towards us. In his left hand he held a sharp knife, gleaming in the sunlight, with a tinge of red on it as if blood had just been wiped off its blade.

Trembling with fear, I pursed my lips and began to whistle.

'Jambo!' I said loudly, quivering with fear as he came near.

'Jambo!' His voice sounded like the trumpeting of a wild rogue elephant. 'You've come to see the lake?'

'Yes.' My eyes were still fixed on his knife.

'There is a wazungu's farm nearby, bwana.' It seemed as if that illiterate rustic had at once read my thoughts. 'He sometimes asks me to slaughter his sheep for him. They are very well-bred sheep.'

Running his tongue over his lips when he looked at me with hunger in his eyes, I felt I too was a well-bred, extremely delectable sheep.

'Cigarette?' I asked, lighting one for myself, as though bleating like a helpless sheep under his knife.

'No bwana, these luxuries are not meant for the likes of us poor people. But yes, if you give me a couple of cents, it's fine.' He saw me put my hand in my pocket and addressed Ma ji and my wife very respectfully.

'Sante bwana kuba! Sante saana,' he said thanking us as he took the samuni from me. From the trumpeting of a wild elephant, he was now yelping like a pet dog. And I drew upon the cigarette and confidently walked ahead.

Mercilessly trampled by our feet, the mud track just seemed to lose its breadth at one point.

'This is Lake Kikuyu.'

In front of us, a little distance away appeared a chunk of wet earth which seemed like a child suddenly smiling through its sobs, as if reassured by our bafflement.

'Yes, bwana kuba, this is Lake Kikuyu. On the surface you only see land but just below it, the water is several miles deep.'

'Very strange.' As I looked at this strange phenomenon, my eyes fell on yet another strange sight. An American girl with a few tourist friends was jumping about on the trembling land resting on the water. 'How strange this is!'

'Look over there, you can see several puddles. Some of them are partially covered by a layer of mud, but there are also some that are so deep that if anyone falls into them, he'll vanish without a trace.'

Sitting near us was a middle-aged Gujarati couple. The man addressed me, 'These black urchins know this lake every inch. They jump into one puddle and come out of another.'

'Really?'

'If you throw a samuni into them, these fellows will bring it out immediately.'

The Gujarati seth reached into the inside of his coat to make sure that his wallet had not been nicked by these people. 'Very clever fellows…these rascals.'

We too tried to find some place to sit down right there. 'Can you go down into these puddles?' I asked one African boy.

'Two years ago this boy's older brother jumped in for one shilling,' another black boy started telling me, 'and right in front of our eyes, he got sucked into the water and just vanished who knows where.'

A stream trickled out of his little brother's eyes just like the streams that were erupting from the wet earth, below the grass.

'Don't you feel scared when you go down?'

'No, bwana,' they said in a chorus, laughing. The younger brother too wiped his tears and tried to laugh. 'No, bwana.'

'Come on, now sit down all of you and eat,' my wife said to the children, opening the tiffin carrier. 'We'll take you down to the lake after that.'

'All that walking has made me really hungry.'

I quickly rolled up an egg into a roti and started gobbling it down.

'What's the hurry? You're such a kid.'

As I was gulping down the food, I happened to glance at the African children. They were sitting quietly in a huddle like old men and staring at us. When it is not wrong for boys to become old men, then for old men to become children is considered right. Just like a child, I pleaded to my wife, 'This curry is too little. Give me more.'

When we had had our fill, before washing the utensils the African boys distributed the leftovers amongst themselves.

'How will this be enough for these poor kids?' I asked my wife, 'give them those sweets as well.'

'And if our children feel hungry after a little while, what will I give them?'

'You seem to be very kind, babu,' the Gujarati seth said to me.

'Ji?' I said, as if I had not heard what he said.

'I said you appear to be very kind-hearted.'

After your belly is full, if you come across someone who praises you, the heart brims over with pleasure.

'You are right, Seth ji, my son is truly a noble soul.'

My wife carefully put away the packet of sweets into another basket. And I blushed with embarrassment, telling myself with a smile, Seth ji is right and so is Ma ji, absolutely right.

Then I lay down and, lighting a cigarette, asked the seth casually, 'Where in Nairobi do you live, Seth ji?'

A little later, the children had started clamouring to go down to the lake.

When we stepped on the earth over the lake, we found it moving under our feet. With that, our hearts too felt the tremor. But we went ahead with a smile, slowly and carefully at first. And when we had overcome our fear, soon we were laughing and jumping like the others with carefree minds.

'How strange is this!' Like a schoolboy, I jumped about on the quivering earth.

'This lake too is a mojaza — a great miracle of Nature, see.' Drawing my wife's attention to myself, I jumped up even higher. Beneath my steps, the earth trembled, just like the heart of a poor African, on which innumerable sorrows leap and burst out into guffaws.

The boi, who works in some Asian diplomat's magnificent bungalow (It is two years since I saw my little Zayi, I wonder what she looks like now?)...

The black labourer works painstakingly to put up paintings by a blonde... English artist for an exhibition, (This work will be completed by the evening. What will I do tomorrow?)

This young and intelligent scion of an indigent African family, studying in the technical college! (Myaoon, if you don't pay your fees by tomorrow, your name will be struck off the college rolls. Myaoon wants to bark like a dog, but can only lick empty milk vessels like a sick and hapless cat. Myaaaoon, myaaaaa ooon!)

My wife was saying to me, 'You won't find such a wonder anywhere else in the world.' What she was actually trying to tell me was that had her parents not brought me to this country, I would not have had the good fortune of seeing such wonders. 'Look!' she said, bouncing on the trembling earth.

'Hai Ram!' She spun around quickly on hearing Harish's scream. Harish had fallen into a small pit while he was running.

It seemed as if the ditch had raised its head through the tall grass and was very respectfully saying to us 'don't be scared, how can lowly creatures like us bring harm to you?'

One of the African boys who had come with us quickly jumped into the ditch and rescued Harish, and said to me with his pleading eyes, 'Saheb, bakshish?'

I took out a couple of copper coins and placed them on his palm.

'Sat Naam! Thanks to you, our Saviour. Beta, go to the temple today itself and make an offering of one maund of grains there.'

'Come on, let's head back now.' My wife held Harish tightly in her arms.

'Ma, Coca Cola!' Sobbing Harish expressed a wish.

'Why? It is not all that dangerous. We won't go any further, let's stay here for a little longer,' I protested.

All of us settled down on the newly-cut grass lying on the side. Just then, we heard the sharp and sweet voice of the young American tourist from nearby.

'How deep is this pit?'

'Very deep, memsaheb,' an African boy replied.

'Okay, we will throw a shilling into it, you go retrieve it. Here's one two, three…' she counted out six more coins and said, 'Now go!'

'No, memsaheb. It's too deep.'

The American tourists laughed and went on their way, while the poor African boy stood there by himself, his greedy eyes staring into the depths of the pit. Nine shillings! Nine! The boy went a little distance away, then came back to the same spot. The boys who were with us too went and stood beside him. Silently, their fearful eyes were measuring the depth of the pit, looking for the nine shiny coins in its unknown depth.

Finally, with great sadness and frustration they walked away, shaking their heads in despair, as if it was not the American girl but they themselves who had lost the nine shillings!

'Ma, Coca Cola.'

After a few minutes I saw a young acquaintance of mine, Mr Yash Vir, coming towards us with his wife.

'Hello!' I called out to him.

'Hello, how are you?'

'So, enjoying your Sunday? Come, join us, and sit down!'

'No, we'll wander around a bit.' But when his wife sat down next to my wife, he also came and sat down beside me.

'So have you settled down now? Are you happy?' I asked. Yash Vir had come to Kenya for the first time a few months ago, and was teaching at a school in Nairobi.

'One begins to like this place effortlessly, ji. Such first-class beautiful scenery all around.' But quickly, bringing a tone of superiority in his voice, he said, 'But there's one thing...the cultural and social life of this country is very poor. Not like our cities at all.'

Mrs Vir was saying to my wife, 'Look at Mr Vir, he's not like other boys from India...he is so smart. He looks just like a local young man.' Mrs Yash Vir was born and brought up in Kenya. When her father could not find a suitable, well-educated boy for her here, he took her to India for marriage.

'You are absolutely right,' I said to Mr Yash Vir, 'the cultural standards here are really low!' I said this as if trying to convince Yash Vir that I was very cultured.

'Vinay Saheb is always full of praise for you. We must make it a point to meet. One hardly meets intelligent people here.'

'Sure, sure, of course,' I said, very pleased. 'Vinay Saheb praises you, too. He is an old friend of mine. In Delhi, he and I used to go to Chandni Chowk every evening to have chaat.'

'Oh, what can one say about that chaat! No matter how much you have, it's never enough. And look at this place, no one can make decent chaat here. What kind of a country is this?'

'Forget about this place. No one knows anything here. What I propose is: the salary should be of this place and one should be living in Delhi. That would be fun.'

'That would indeed be perfect. I am getting 800 shillings per month on arrival.'

'I get 1400 including house allowance,' I said this slightly loudly so that his wife would also hear me.

'But you know, sister, one doesn't know where all that money goes,' my wife said to Mrs Yash Vir.

For a moment my mind started calculating my bank balance. 'Yash ji, what you say is right. There is something missing in life here, it is not the same wonderful culture.'

My three children started prancing about us. Like a schoolmaster, Yash Vir told them to sit down quietly, and then he himself stood up and started jumping with them. One by one, all of us had started jumping and leaping about, and even Ma ji was swinging her legs while sitting! Gasping and trembling, the earth was breathless.

'Haha haha!'

The African boys stared at us silently.

'What a miracle this is!'

'Truly, you would never find such a lake anywhere in the world.'

'The eighth wonder of the world.'

'Come, let's go further up and walk around a bit,' Mrs Yash Vir said to her husband.

'Yes, let's go to the shore.'

'Let's take everything along, someone might run away with our stuff,' my wife suggested.

'Very well.'

On reaching the shore of the lake, all of us stood on one side in a group. Nearby, a middle-aged African man was sitting under a tree, engrossed in reading a newspaper. I walked up to him. He gave me a bitter, questioning look.

In a very friendly voice, I said to him, 'Below out feet, the earth above the lake trembles and shakes. What a miracle this is.'

Very dryly the African responded, 'But what I consider a miracle is the fact that only the earth above the lake shakes under your feet, and not the whole of Africa.'

'Sat Naam Shri Wahe Guru!'

Translated by Keerti Ramchandra

Seeking Answers

•

Sab ka Sawal

A nd once more, afraid and trembling, he would start sliding on the gleeful edges of the future. Even in one's imagination, falling from these steep edges one would lose one's life without a gasp.

Not to say that the chant developing slowly in his soul would promptly step in to save him. Or else intoxicated by such happy desires the poor dejected fellow, even when committing suicide, could believe that immortality in the form of a shy bride is approaching him hesitatingly…as though the moment had finally come to quench his thirst for such desires.

If Makoji's chants too had felt dejected and had surrendered, he would have been baffled and, by now, he'd have probably committed suicide. But Makoji's faith remained strong; he remained alive and kept mumbling drunkenly, like one who knows he is intoxicated. That's all.

'I …my…' Even without listening to his trembling voice I knew what he was saying, because for the past five years or so I had been hearing the same story.

'I have saved some amount of money. Will collect some more in the next four-five years. And then I will resign from this lousy job. His voice would throb with pleasure at the thought of giving up his 'lowly job'. 'Yes, I will quit then and I will go to Lincoln's Inn, London, to become a barrister…' He'd stop there and his face would light up as he imagined his successful foray into London.

'When I return wearing the barrister's gown from Lincoln's Inn and take up all those big cases in court, people will marvel at my eloquence. Then you will be proud to be my friend. It's just a matter of a couple of years before I resign from here.'

'Mwangi, yaar, our boss is very unhappy these days. I sometimes wonder if we'll actually be thrown out of jobs one of these days.'

I would smile, because he would get very agitated, as though his aspirations were crying like some poor orphaned children. But his innocent blind faith would reassure those children. 'Looks like you too have started laughing at me like the others, Mwangi. I feel sorry that you dismiss the bright future which I am waiting for, which must come for my sake... The day when I will live, not to strive for my boss's approval, but for my own sake. I will become a barrister and ensure that law and justice are upheld.'

My pessimism was defeated by his innocence and it would slink away and, with our heads together, we would sit for hours, gazing into the rising sun of a bright and happy future. We would then feel reassured and begin to live for ourselves.

'I have saved some amount.' Once again we would snap back into the real world, despairing, dejected, and helpless. 'I will save some more, and then you see, my friend...'

I watched uninterrupted but Makoji's story, instead of moving forward, remained entangled in the same beaten up incidents, giggling and smirking.

Our tables were alongside each other in the railway office. Very often Makoji would stop working, and he would be lost gazing at a picture on the wall in front of him. In the picture, there was a poor African child standing on a heap of rags strewn on the ground, his bright eyes dancing up and down the vast slopes and heights of a distant mountain. It seemed as if the child was about to run up and reach the peaks of that mountain. But for many years we had seen the child standing right there, amidst the rags. The happiness in his eyes was mocking at the helplessness of the child.

Oh, these mountains, these lofty heights! You fool, these heights are way out of your reach. Come let us play around at the foot of the mountain and be happy...

'No, no. I wish to go right up...look there, around those peaks.'

'Look, son,' Father Jacob, an extremely kind English teacher, often used to say to Makoji, 'you are a very intelligent boy. If you wish to scale those peaks you must work really hard. A man reaps the fruit of what he sows.'

Makoji had sown the seeds of his golden childhood dreams with great love and effort. When the result of his school certificate examination was declared, these seeds had sprouted into tender young saplings with long shoots and green leaves. He was thrilled to see himself get a first division, but how could he quench his thirst before this young tree had borne its fruit? That is why he had to survive by devouring the leaves of the young trees like an animal. If he were not to be a clerk in the railways, who would repay his deceased father's debt? Who would take care of his widowed sister and his nieces and nephews? Who knows how many times the youthful golden dreams of Makoji wept, but he continued to feed on those leaves, to clear his father's debt, to wipe the tears of his widowed sister. Some times when he was free of these preoccupations, he would stand by the window of his heart, draw aside the curtain and look deep within.

This plane is flying toward London. This is the London airport, This, Lincoln's Inn... Lincoln's Inn, welcoming its new students with a legally correct smile and words of encouragement. This well-dressed boy is the son of an African chieftain who rules over thirteen settlements; this, the carefree scion of a wealthy Indian businessman, whose pockets are full of new currency notes; that ponderous youngster, whose father is an African-English officer, who will become an even bigger officer after studying law here... And then this one... And that one ...and then he...but Makoji is not amongst them, Makoji who was one of the best students of his school. People who heard his arguments in debates would often exclaim 'this boy was born to be a lawyer'. But boys born for the legal profession do not study jurisprudence at Lincoln's Inn; instead, they become routine grade clerks in some railway office.

Sitting beside me, Makoji would be adding up huge sums of money in the ledger. Tired, he would hold his head in both his hands and fix his lost eyes on the picture hanging in front, on the opposite wall. Who knows where he reached this way?

Sometimes, during this while, my eyes met his and he looked embarrassed with a kind of guilt on his face. He would say, 'I haven't given up hope yet, Mwangi. I never will. You wait and see.'

And then one day, I unexpectedly received transfer orders from headquarters... Four hundred miles away from the familiar lanes of my homeland to an unknown coast, where the earth dives into the ocean to lie deep down like a corpse.

There were just a few minutes left for the train to leave the station. My friend Makoji's deeply sad silence was – as it were – making a half-hearted conversation as he looked at me. 'Go Mwangi, Khuda Hafiz...but I wonder, to whom will I open my heart now?'

I went up to him and embraced him. 'Makoji, my dear brother, forget about being a barrister and all that. Live your life with a smile and a song. When small people like us have big dreams and make them the goals of our lives, even our small pleasures are snatched away, and we die unfulfilled.' My words became blows hitting at him.

'Forgive me, my friend, I am truly sorry. I admire your determination, but I sincerely want you to be cheerful and happy always.'

He made a feeble attempt to smile. 'Oh don't worry, the day is not far when you will see this friend of yours always laughing and joking. It's not only a matter of my words or my destiny, it is a test of my patience. Let me face this test my friend, I have already saved something, a little more needs to be ...' As the guard's whistle screeched hysterically, mocking at him, I bid him good bye and got on the train. Sometimes it so happens that while one is separated from one's dear ones only for a little bit, one is not able to meet them for several years. The element of chance takes over a person's hopes, and he remains helplessly looking. For a while I used to wait eagerly for Makoji's letters. Then this phase came to an end. In the meantime, I got married, had a family, the children grew up, and one of them even started working. Twenty years went by.

Last month my team was conducting a series of inspections of several small stations under the supervision of an Englishman. One morning as our train sped towards Kikuyu station, I don't know why but Makoji's face kept flashing before my eyes. The same face of twenty years ago – his delusory eyes, trapped in the web of some uncertain future, the deep inky hue of his hopeful face, the thick, tangled curls, and the perfectly fleshy and ever-quivering African lips.

'Makoji, my friend, where are you?' I felt like flying to his side, wherever he was. Suddenly, I felt guilty for not having kept in touch with my friend all these years. Makoji's dejected, despairing words echoed in my head. 'Go, Mwangi, Khuda Hafiz... I wonder, to whom will I open my heart out now?'

Who doesn't build castles in the sand in childhood, but who keeps thinking of these castles in adulthood?

When the train jolted to a halt at Kikuyu station, I remembered my dear friend and made up my mind to find his address somehow, and go meet him. I got off the train and my heart danced with joy like some happy spirit when I saw a familiar face on the platform. I quickly walked up to him. Makoji!

My heart rose to my lips, but no words came out. Instead, I just hugged him tight for a long moment. Silently, I savoured the happiness, counting the thudding beats of my heart. I was surprised at my unbridled joy. Very often, as we tread on new paths, we temporarily forget the old and familiar roads. But if fate takes us down on those roads again, the smell of that earth leaves us speechless with prodigious delight and love.

Oh, you.

You...!

What could be a happier coincidence than our meeting this way? My dream to see Makoji had come alive and was standing stretched before me.

Kikuyu Railway Station was under Makoji's charge. His house, a short distance away, beckoned me with open arms. His children were playing in the courtyard outside; his middle-aged wife smiled shyly, and then looking at both of us, she left all that she was busy with and looked at her husband as if asking with her eyes, 'who is this man?'

'Ari, this is Mwangi, my friend, my brother, my everything...'

After I saw Makoji's cheerful home, his devoted wife and his growing children, I felt a certain kind of satisfaction. The young man I remembered from a long time ago, driven by a false hope, had got lost somewhere. He had wrapped his sorrowful song in the shroud of practicality.

'Okay,' she smiled.

I was very happy to see my friend in this content state. He seemed to be very content in the present circumstance.

Different from the Makoji of old times. 'Okay...' I put my arm around his shoulders and accompanied him into the sitting room. Several thick books lay haphazardly on a table in a corner. There was also a big shelf, again full of books... Roman Law, British Law, International Law, Law and Justice... They seemed to be loudly mocking at my happiness, like stubborn children dancing and teasing me noisily. Bewildered, I looked at my friend.

He laughed. 'I have read all these books, even memorized most of them.' His laughter seemed to be laced with tears. 'I have managed to save some money. I will put together some more, then after three-four years I will retire and go off to England. It's just a matter of a few days now.'

Just then one of Makoji's young sons playing outside the quarters started crying loudly, as if representing his father's dreams.

For so long has this continued as a futile hope. Spreading along the banks of the future, that same quivering voice of a lunatic, echoing and falling...it was the same old Makoji.

My mind went into the future and I saw Makoji lying on his deathbed, and death beckoning him from above his head... And he, in a semi coma, staring at the wall in front of him with his ever-hopeful eyes, muttering, 'See, just a little more remains...Once that is done, I will leave for England at once... Lincoln's Inn, Samuel Makoji, Bar-at-Law... Bar-at-...'. And Makoji closes his eyes forever. But longevity, like a bashful bride, moves forward on hesitant feet. As if after death the moment of extinguishing of the flame of his aspirations has finally arrived.

And then in my imagination, late Makoji's spirit actually becomes a barrister and enters God's court wearing the elegant black gown of Lincoln's Inn.

'Milord, I, the soul of late Makoji, in the capacity of a responsible barrister, am present in this divine court to file an extremely important case on humanitarian grounds.' Makoji's soul, examining his surroundings like a lawyer, looks around seeking support. 'Your Honour, humanity seeks an answer from its Creator, the Almighty, as to why man is so helpless and poor, and why does he have to wait till his death to realize his dreams?'

Translated by Keerti Ramchandra

The Slump

·

Manda

T he patrons of the United Club of Nairobi took great
pleasure in being known as affluent intellectuals. They paid
approximately 30 pounds a year to gorge on the mutton samosas
in the club's garden restaurant, sat listening to conversations
between the rich and powerful in the big hall, had a weekly
dinner, and every evening mingled with the other members at
the bar, totting up a hefty bill while presenting their contrarian
opinions on various topics.

According to the rules of the club, people of all races and
communities could become its members. But, in truth, the
blacks were represented only by the club's African waiters. At
the last General Body Meeting, an Asian member had raised
the issue and asked a European Committee Member about why
African people did not like to become members at the club.
After pondering on the gravity of this query, the High Council
had finally reached the conclusion that Africans had not yet
become civilized enough. Therefore, they were still bereft of
the niceties required to lead a socially fit life.

Every time a new member set foot in this large hall of the
club, he slowed down, hesitated, and his voice dropped to a
whisper. Such was the sight that greeted him – of old members,
spiffy in their rich garments and full of elaborate gestures. But
once he mingled with them for a while his image sat well with
theirs, and he became part of a very happy frame. When dear

Mrs Becky runs through the list of merits of a pickle that she has made all by herself, he also relishes the mischief dancing in her eyes. Whenever the tall, middle-aged Bull starts off about his department's service to the nation, he begins to look at him in wonder and admiration. While listening to the useless son of the richest man of the city – Narayan ji – holding forth, he would assure him that the entire country would very soon be forced to acknowledge him as a path-bearer. And finally, when all the members would be delighted at his behaviour, he would return their intimate looks as if to say, 'Now you too say something complimentary about me.'

'Ashofi Saheb, your observation is very deep indeed.'

'Ashofi Saheb, read your analysis in *The Kenya Times*. Till date, I haven't ever seen a better essay on economics.'

'Ashofi Saheb, it's amazing how well you shave. Which blade do you use?'

When people turn away from lesser gods and begin to venerate one Supreme God, the earthly entities begin to worship each other amongst themselves.

As was their wont, everyone was present at the club that day. When Harmuz ji, sitting at the left-hand corner close to the bar counter, lost his hand at cards, he bought every member of the group a double peg of whisky in keeping with their agreed wager.

'Arré, Harmuz ji,' Radha Krishna, sitting at another table with another group, headed their way urgently, waving a newspaper at them. 'Look at this, Harmuz ji,' he thrust the newspaper forward, 'Shyam ji Heer ji have gone bankrupt.'

'Bankrupt?' Doctor Inam asked, raising his whisky glass to his lips in no seeming hurry. He was already thinking of how, perhaps, Shyam ji would very soon suffer a heart attack and send for his services. 'How unfortunate.' He appeared extremely displeased at realizing that his whisky glass was suddenly empty.

'Shyam ji is a very smart man.' Harmuz ji took his eyes off the newspaper. 'Even in this state of bankruptcy he has profited by 15,000 pounds.'

'How's that?'

'Two or three months back, he had deposited this amount under the name of his eldest son and sent it out of the colony.' Harmuz ji had already made up his mind about opening up an account in a bank in England in his wife's name. He turned his loving gaze upon his wife to encounter her loving gaze upon Narayan ji's youthful, unemployed son's luscious hair as she enquired sweetly why he no longer visited their home.

'Why are so many Asian companies facing bankruptcy these days?'

'You do not understand Mr Goodluck, the traders are suffering very badly these days.' Radha Krishna suddenly felt crushed like an insect, flowing away with the tide. His firm was facing severe losses for some months now. 'We have witnessed a trade slump like this for the first time in the colony. There are men everywhere, swarming, but you cannot see a single buyer.'

'Yes, there is indeed a slump these days,' Narayan ji's son piped in, 'my father was mentioning that at least twenty workers will be laid off in our factory soon, three Europeans and seventeen Asians. Mr. Goodluck, your glass is empty. Boy!'

'In our post office, ninety men will be relieved next month,' said Mr Goodluck, a high-ranking official at the GPO. 'God alone knows how this slump has descended upon us so suddenly.'

'This is a massive slump Mr Hardstone,' Ashofi Saheb began, 'today, countries across the world are surviving only because they are supporting each other. In my opinion, it is because of the current trade slump in England and America…

that has affected our condition.' Ashofi Saheb looked all around, his haughty, self-admiring eyes checking out the faces before finally colliding with dear Mrs Veni's impish ones, barely managing to steady themselves. 'Why has Mr Veni not come to the club today, Mrs Veni?'

Mrs Veni responded, 'He has an important case at the court tomorrow, he's preparing for it,' as if to say 'how does his absence matter, your presence here is enough'.

Ashofi Saheb's joy knew no bounds, 'But you must believe me when I say that this slump will not last forever.'

'When I first arrived here in 1950...' It was Shamsher Singh's habit to listen to his own voice very keenly, 'You could not spot even a single poor person.' An African waiter, acting on unspoken orders, came and stood before Shamsher Singh with a cup of coffee laced with brandy. 'You would not spot a single poor person, no one was unemployed and, in fact, it was difficult to find people to do your work. But today, even for an ordinary post, there are twenty applicants running around to get it.'

'How well I speak in English,' Shamsher Singh's mind began its familiar self-praise, 'how amazingly well! Each one of these people seem to be deeply enamoured by my eloquence in the language.'

'You are right Mr Singh. My last month was wasted entirely in selecting suitable candidates for two of my clients. My eyes were so tired from reading the applications. Every day someone or the other would land up at my bungalow with a recommendation. Now you tell me, how long can a man who gets two thousand as salary waste his time on these trivial matters?' The speaker's gaze darted from person to person, as if saying 'I take home a monthly salary of two thousand did you hear that?' Then he sat back and relaxed, lighting his American cigar and puffing away deeply at it with satisfaction.

'Yes, but from where has this chill crept into the market?' Ram Krishna blurted, bewildered by his losses. He picked up his glass and emptied it of the Stout in a big gulp.

'In my opinion this is not a massive slump, according to the rules of trade.'

The glass of Stout ran its course through Ram Krishna's body and made him anxious. He interrupted Ashofi Saheb, 'But what is the real lesson in all this?'

'The real lesson?' Narayan ji's son unfurled himself and stood up, completely under the influence of his whisky. He turned to Mrs Harmuz, 'What is a real lesson Mrs Harmuz ji? Today you must absolutely explain the meaning of a real lesson to me.'

Mrs Harmuz ji gently coaxed him back to his seat and began to play lovingly with his beautiful locks.

Harmuz ji looked upon both of them and decided that the new bank account in England was certainly not going to be in his wife's name.

'Mr Ram Krishna,' he said, 'the real lesson of this slump is that we can no longer trust each other as we used to.'

'Now we can see our future before us.'

'The market has grown far more competitive.'

'We are losing our money.'

'No politics please.'

'But I insist on asking, what is the true lesson of this slump?' Ram Krishna wanted to place another order for whisky but he remembered that he had invited his income tax advisor home for dinner. A five-year old tax return had got into a problem. He rose up to leave, 'I still do not understand the real learning from this slump.'

When all the members of the club had left one by one in their cars, then the African servers quickly finished the rest of their chores and collected together at the servant's quarters. Mesuki looked around at all of them smiling impishly, and fished out a bottle which all the bearers of the club had quietly topped up with the leftover drinks from the members' glasses.

'Lozego, let us begin.'

'There's quite a fill of cocktail here today.'

'Harmuz ji's memsaheb did not even touch her last peg today.'

'Once her fingers begin to dance in that boy's hair, she usually forgets her pegs.'

'That rascal Hardstone doesn't leave even a drop.'

The waiters all began to pour out the cocktail into their glasses.

'Matele, Goodluck's memsaheb is a very interesting woman, much more so than food.'

'Why aren't our women like them, friend?'

'It's the perfume they wear, buddy, but this woman is naturally attractive. Living a carefree life makes even a sheep look wondrous.'

'Forget it, what's all this you are talking about,' the old Metheka couldn't stop himself. 'Talk about something important, Mesoki, what is this slump they were talking about? The sahebs were saying that a huge slump has hit our country.'

'Slump?' The half-drunk Mesoki was thinking 'let me empty my glass and then I can explain to them what this word means'.

'These people were only talking about their own businesses, rafiqui,' Maragori said.

'I think this slump must be something really attractive that people are drinking double the usual amount.'

'Mesoki, please tell us, what is this slump?'

Mesoki quickly emptied his glass, wiped his lips and pouring more of the cocktail into the glass, he smiled.

'Old man, a slump is a downward trend, a fall in the market. These people are saying that a huge fall in the market has hit our country.' Mesoki raised his glass to his lips again.

'Ha, ha, ha, a loss, ha, ha…' Matele guffawed. He often said that his mind became sharper every time he sat laughing and drinking with his friends.

'Now you tell me, friends, for how long have you seen this slump?' Matele questioned, as if asking himself. Then his eyes swelled up with a deep sadness, and he seemed like a bloated corpse floating on the surface of still waters.

'Friends, our masters, the bwanas, say the slump has hit us today, but I have been seeing it coming for many years, from even before 1930. While scrubbing the dirty utensils of a trader I used to wonder why my parents didn't keep me with themselves in the village.…'

Translated by Chandana Dutta

When Life Dies

•

Jab Zindagi Mar Jati Hai

At the break of dawn, the middle-aged Thomas Jaroge was rubbing his eyes and waking up but since old habits die hard, he shut his eyes to pray, keeping to his twenty-year-old routine, 'O Lord! Let my eyes be always open so that I can see Your work around me, marvel at its beauty and be grateful to You for it all. Amen!'

He opened his eyes, looked lovingly at his wife and children lying close to him, got up and said jambo to his mother who was coughing in the adjacent room. Stepping out of his government quarters he turned on the tap, started brushing his teeth and sang a sacred hymn under his breath.

> *He will not his great self deny:*
> *A God all truth can never lie;*
> *As soon might he his Being quit*
> *As break his oath, or word forget.*

> *True to his word, God gave his Son,*
> *To die for crimes which men had done*
> *Blest pledge! He never will revoke*
> *A single promise he has spoke.'*

Turning in her bed in the quarter next door, young Kotino muttered, 'This son of God neither sleeps himself...nor lets others sleep!'

Soon, Jaroge had bathed and was ready. By then, all members of the family were up and about too. His wife got busy preparing breakfast in the kitchen, and creating quite a ruckus, the two older kids started getting ready for school. His old mother's coughing ceased. She made Zayi, her eighteen-month-old granddaughter, sit on her bed and started playing with her. It appeared as though just then, a fairy with a magic wand had touched that lifeless, old dwelling with light all around, and the still character of the house started to throb with life on its own. It had woken up laughing to play the game of hide and seek with life itself.

Wiping the lens of his glasses, Jaroge adjusted his spectacles and looked around smiling, as though saying, 'What a lucky creature man is! What a lucky creature I am!'

Shaking his head with satisfaction, he went into the kitchen to help his wife, 'Come, I'll take care of tea – you make toast.'

Looking lovingly at his wife, he said, 'You know what Modia... I think if you were not Modia you would be Jaroge. And because you're not Jaroge, you're Modia. You tell me... what is the difference between the two of us?'

Pressing his left arm against Modia's right, he looked deep into her eyes as though wanting to say, 'We're the parents of our children, Modia. These children are the little songs of our love...they're like hymns in the Bible which validate our very existence.'

'Modia, one never dies because one's ripe old years get transformed by getting absorbed into the young smiles of one's children; one becomes fresh all over again and gets rejuvenated.'

At this point his daughter Zayi started crying and Jaroge ran to her side and held her against him. 'No my darling, shhhh... my little girl is an angel, my little girl is a beautiful little girl, she's very...'

Jaroge's old mother smiled, 'You're an old man now Jaroge but still a total kid. Such sweet talk is liked by children only on a full belly.' She then called out to Modia, 'Is the milk ready for Zayi or not?'

As soon the bottle of milk touched her lips, Zayi settled down and looking at her father's face, her sparkling eyes seemed to say, 'Now tell me Abbi, what were you saying?'

Wiping the tears from his daughter's eyes, Jaroge said to her lovingly, 'My Zayi is an angel, my little girl is very beautiful, she's very…'

Zayi held her father's nose and laughed with joy as though saying, 'Baba, you're such a kid…'

When Jaroge stepped out of the house to go to office, a bright and promising day saluted him. Feeling one with its beauty and brilliance, Jaroge whole-heartedly embraced it. Outside, life seemed very fresh, extremely cheerful, free of the day's worries and ready.

'Come on, come on…don't just stand there and stare! Nothing ventured, nothing gained. No one here gets a prize without working for it.' Jaroge started thinking about his prize of four hundred and fifty shillings per month, a government quarter to live in and benevolent bosses!

This was his prize for the hard work he'd put in for twenty-five long years of worthy employment. On the first day of every month when he put his earnings on the palm of middle-aged Modia, his eyes would be shining with youthful fervour. His aged mother was overjoyed and thought had his father been alive today, he'd have been swept off his feet with happiness. Poor fellow had spent all his life lamenting in abject poverty.

Four hundred and fifty shillings! With this salary, he bought milk for Zayi, took care of the health and education of his children and also bought peace of mind for himself and his family. And after buying all this, he would still be left with a couple of pounds per month. Life was worth its while, secure and stable.

Walking briskly on the road, Jaroge's eyes would say to fellow-walkers, 'Come on, if like me you also want to get a prize, then cheerfully get into this race….come on…'

Suddenly, Jaroge tripped and almost fell on his face. Catching his breath he slowed down a little.

For many years now Jaroge had been walking on this path every day, covering the distance which carried the happy picture of people's untiring struggle. For the welfare of humankind, this presented shining models of selfless service. Jaroge and this road knew each other well and were old friends since the time when in childhood, the half-clad little Jaroge brought his father's goats to graze here on the naked chest of the road. Now this land too had covered its identity with a magnificent European attire. And Jaroge too had worn a coat and pants.

The City Square! That statue of the city's first European City Engineer! There he was, standing and gazing at the city's beautiful styles of architecture, smiling with a triumphant posture. Around the square stood hordes of high-rise buildings, as if pondering over people's grand resolutions with a sense of wonder and appreciation.

On reaching the Municipal Hospital building, Jaroge slowed down. The beautiful garden and the vibrant flowers extended a cheerful welcome to each new patient. 'Wearing clean, sterilized aprons, the physicians here are continuously engaged in attending to patients…and the innocent beauty of the nurses cheerfully sucks the sting of the patients' pain.' Jaroge recalled the time two years ago, when he was brought here while struggling between life and death. In his mind, he once again thanked all the hospital staff who had saved Modia from being widowed, his small children from being orphaned and his old mother from losing her only support. His eyes welled up with gratitude and appreciation.

On reaching the Roman Catholic Church, Jaroge bowed his head reverentially. 'The dome of this church seems to be pointing towards the wide open blue, as if showing some path. On that path is suspended a very big cross. From that cross flows a stream of Jesus Christ's blood that feeds the smiles of humanity.'

'Good morning, Father!'

'Good morning, Jaroge!' The priest seemed to be in a hurry but seeing Jaroge, he stopped. 'Tell me, how is Modia?'

'She is well, Father.'

'She was absent for the service in the church last Sunday. You must bring her with you, son.'

How concerned the shepherd is about his flock!

Now Jaroge had reached Nano's restaurant. Nano was his childhood friend, and this tiny restaurant of his was a living memory of Jaroge's forgotten stinginess and youth. In those days when he was without a job for a couple of years, he would come running here to eat chakula, eggs, and chicken as though this was his mother's kitchen.

Every day, Nano would light two cigarettes and offer one to his friend while holding back one between his fingers. And then Jaroge would lecture him while Nano sulked as he suffered the words of wisdom.

'Nano, yesterday you were drunk and falling all over the place in the park again?'

'So what rafiqui...I was only falling all over...I didn't kill anyone, did I?'

'It's now time you sorted out the goal of your life, Nano.'

'Look, Jaroge, you keep sorting out the goal while I enjoy life. The goal is not all there is to it, you see…!'

Walking past Nano's shop, Jaroge thought, 'My friend is bit of a happy-go-lucky chap but he has a heart of gold.' Making a cross on his chest, he prayed to the Lord that the world may never be bereft of good souls like Nano.

Just five hundred yards short of the office, Jaroge's eyes would start looking for the crippled fakir who'd be sitting on a sheet spread out under the mango tree every day at that time. And every day, Jaroge got tremendous satisfaction in giving him a samuni, and was further gratified by the blessings showered upon him. At that moment, Jaroge would want to cast aside all false differences of class and embrace him.

Today also, Jaroge's eyes turned towards the tree but not finding the beggar there, his eyes wandered around. Standing right under the tree Jaroge felt that even though the fakir was not physically present there, his spirit was looking for alms with outstretched hands. Jaroge's spirit today kept a shining samuni there instead of a cent.

One soul blessed another.

'May the Lord keep your name alive, always.'

Jaroge's soul smiled on hearing this.

'A man's name will live, always.'

'May your plants be evergreen.'

'The Lord has promised in the Holy Book that all plants shall be evergreen.'

'May this samuni come back to you as 500 shillings.'

'This is the will of the Lord. Charity returns as prosperity.'

Jaroge was visibly happy as he entered the office gate almost as though the board at the gate bearing the name of the office had said to him, 'Well done! You are a very good man, well done!'

Feeling the pat on his back Jaroge said to himself, 'Actually we're all very good, every man is a fountain of goodness, selflessness and love, and it is because of these sterling qualities that the beauty of life is breathing.'

A little distance ahead he saw his new boss, the young Mr Albert. Happily, and in a loud and clear voice, Jaroge wished him, 'Good morning, sir!'

Mr Albert turned and looked at him but probably not realizing that Jaroge was addressing him, moved on without responding.

'Mr Albert is such a good person. He's in such a senior position but is completely untouched by any sense of superiority.'

Jaroge was on top of the world.

That afternoon, in the office when everyone sat down to drink tea, the topic of conversation veered around to senior officers.

'Oh, you're talking of that swollen-headed bastard? If I could have my way I'd shoot him down.'

'Everyone knows Pattison, brother. Always frowning, don't know who he thinks he is…the son of a bitch!'

'Today, in the morning, Albert shouted at me for no reason. I gave it back to the bugger till he started cringing!'

'Come on, guys,' Jaroge said gently, looking at all of them. 'What do you get out of bad-mouthing your bosses like this? Why do you stress yourselves out?'

All eyes began talking to each other.

'Bloody sycophant!'

'Slave!'

'He's a dangerous guy!'

Jaroge said, 'Everyone is good in one's own way. If they were to be bad, they wouldn't be human beings.'

'Hypocrite,' another shot was fired at him.

Satisfied, Jaroge smiled and looked at them, convinced that each one of them was now repentant.

There were another few minutes left for the office to close when an attendant came and informed Jaroge that Mr Albert had summoned him. Cheerfully, Jaroge reached Mr Albert's office door but seeing some clerks talking to Mr Albert, he stopped at the door.

'Come in,' Mr Albert said in an authoritative voice.

'Just look at this register, there are at least half a dozen wrong entries here.'

Jaroge smiled, rubbing his palms together as though to apologise.

'If, after twenty-five years of work experience, someone makes stupid mistakes like these...it is the height of irresponsibility.'

Jaroge continued to smile as though saying, 'Mr Albert, you're very nice.'

'I haven't summoned you here to see your smile. You'll have to explain your mistakes.' Jaroge's smile started fading, and a little shaken, he looked at the junior clerks standing on one side of the room.

'I have received other reports too that indicate that your work is becoming increasingly unsatisfactory.'

Jaroge's smile at once vanished and he stammered, 'But...but...'

'No ifs and buts now. Listen to me carefully, I don't need non-performers here.'

'Non-performers!' It was as though the young officer had hit the old chin of Jaroge with his shining, well-polished shoes.

'I don't need non-performers here.' It felt as though the silence of the junior clerks standing close by was making fun of him through their loud laughter.

Returning home from office he heard a clerk saying, 'Mr Albert is really good-hearted.'

'Good-hearted?' Jaroge was grinding his teeth.

On the way back, the empty space under the mango tree seemed to inform him that the beggar hadn't been there all day.

'Maybe…maybe he has suddenly died.' And instead of the thought making him sad, his lips arched into a cruel smile.

Going forward, he stopped at the next turn. Every day on his way back he used to take the road to the right going past Nano's shop, then the Roman Catholic Church, and then via the Municipal Hospital he would reach his house.

Looking at his usual route hesitatingly, he sulked and took a different road today.

As he reached home, his faithful wife, the middle-aged Modia, welcomed him with a radiant smile belying her years, but this irritated Jaroge and he thought when a woman starts aging she should not try to look young and exhibit herself this way.

With her innocent eyes, Zayi lovingly looked at her father and extended her tiny arms, wanting to be picked up. But with a furrowed brow, Jaroge walked past her.

The song of his love, the fruit of his love began to cry and with her little unsteady steps, she came behind Jaroge.

Jaroge turned and looked at her with a piercing look. 'Like a shadow of death, she is always hovering around me,' he cursed.

'Jaroge! Jaroge…son!'

Jaroge felt as though his mother's trembling voice was echoing in a tomb: 'Jaroge!'

But how could the corpse give a reply?

Translated by Vandana R Singh

Land Lust

•

Dharti ka Kaal

Under Khuda's vast open sky, on Lake Saheb's land, his African labourer was warming himself by a fire.

Wrapping his old body in a tattered scruffy blanket closely, Mboya asked in a quivering voice, 'Mendaka, why does one keep thinking about his youth in old age?

'Because the cold troubles him a lot...'

'This blanket is older than me,' said Mboya, pushing a burning twig into the fire. 'Far from keeping me warm, it is pulling away whatever little warmth is left in my bones.'

'My father had not even seen any woollen clothes all his life.'

'Forget about woollen clothes, except for his skin, my father had never worn anything else,' huddling himself deeper into the blanket – as if wanting to snatch away its warmth from it – he replied. 'When he was ninety, a raging fever gripped him and as he was dying, mountains of heat burst out of his body,' said Makanga, rubbing his hands together. 'Well, when Kilimanjaro dada himself is spewing fire, how can my poor little ritualistic practices help?'

For a while, the labourers got distracted from warming themselves. Their eyes sped and went and stood in the lap of Mount Kilimanjaro, across Lake saheb's green fields, beyond wazungu's leased out farmlands way beyond the dense, hazy forests. They had their dwellings there – small thatched huts – where their women folk engaged in their chores could not stop themselves from staring every now and then at Lake saheb's property. Seeing those sad married women, Kilimanjaro's eyes would well up and he would hide his toothless mouth in the dense clouds to weep unabashedly.

'If this year too we get work at the feet of Dada Kilimu, it would be great fun.'

Makhamba's thoughts flew to his brand new bride. For two goats and three sheep, he had been able to marry Patia with great enthusiasm, and the debt for two sheep was still outstanding.

'Makhamba,' Patia's father had warned, 'if the two sheep do not arrive before the toto does, I will take away both the girl and the toto.'

If he had his way, Makhamba would have stretched his neck out, preened like an ostrich and danced before his female, but the two sheep would get entangled between his feet and he would forget the dance and pick up his stick to chase after them.

Menhe menhe…menhe… Running after the sheep had left Makhamba gasping for breath.

'Thoughts of Patia troubling you, Makhamba?'

'Don't get so impatient, rafiqui. First, at least earn a couple of shillings.'

'You're right, Gachru. Wazungu's shilling is more powerful than the shembe.'

Once upon a time, all this land belonged to Kilimu dada. Our small little fields flourished there. All at once, in front of the middle-aged Moaje's dirt-filled eyes floated his childhood– all shining and bright.

'Dada actually belongs to us. Then how come all this land passed into the hands of the wazungu?'

'Come, I will tell you the whole story.' Seeing the elderly Mboya inch closer to the fire, all the others did the same. 'Yeloba, the fire is dying down. Go fetch some dry wood.'

'I am going Mazé, first let me drink this cat blood.'

'So that's what it is. Is that why you are sitting apart from us?'

'Pass some here, Yeloba. If you drink too much, it will be tough on your stomach.'

'Mazé,' Daroro said to Mboya, 'I stole some potatoes from the field today. They are under that tree.'

'Yes, yes, get them. Let's roast them and eat them.' When Daroro went to get the potatoes, Mboya looked at all the men around him. 'Stealing is a very bad thing,' he said to them, 'but if you must steal, never steal potatoes. Quietly pick up a goat or sheep instead. It's been a lifetime since a whole sheep was roasted in the company of friends.'

'I have even forgotten the taste of sheep's meat, Mazé!'

'Don't whine, Dogo, I will get a sheep for you,' Gachru said, 'but our wicked bwana doesn't let a single goat or sheep out of his sight for even a moment.'

'Here, Mazé, potatoes.'

'Put them in the embers. If you ask me, Wazangu, roasted potatoes taste just like sheep.'

'In fact, they are somewhat tastier than sheep meat, Dogo.'

'When wazungu falls ill, he only eats potatoes.'

'You didn't tell us, Mazé, how has our dada's power weakened?'

'After wazungu stuffed himself with potatoes and took all the sheep under his control, what could the old dada do but survive on potatoes?'

'It's a very bad habit you have, Gachru, interrupting like this,' said Mendaka gently admonishing Gachru. Then he turned his attention to Mboya. 'Mazé, Dada Kilimu was so strong that every morning we could hear loud guffaws from the mountain top. Then the sounds became like the continuous rasping cough of uncle Katenga as he leaned over his cot to spit blood. And now even those sounds have stopped altogether.'

'Dada Kilimu couldn't have died, could he?'

'No! Dada Kilimu is our mungu. As long as the earth sprouts posho and heaps of potatoes leap out of their furrows, we must deduce that dada is very much alive.'

'That's right, Dogo, Dada Kilimu can never die. He has become weaker for sure, but he is definitely alive and passing through bad times.'

'Well then, listen Bejago, to your dada's story.' Old Mboya began his narration with child-like innocence.

'My father used to tell this story when I was a child.

At first all this land belonged to our dada. He had entrusted it to us, the black people, and we blacks had established our little settlements here. All around us were dense forests, and Dada Kilimu lived alone on the mountain top.'

'Why did Dada Kilimu live alone, Mazé? Why didn't he come down and live amongst the black people?'

'Because he had very important work up there. Sitting on the peak, he kept an eye on everything around. He protected us, persuaded the heavens to send clouds to our fields, poured rivers of sweet water for us to drink, and made holes in the heart of the mountain so that streams of hot springs would flow down onto those who were ill. I could list them out if they were just a few... But anyway, listen further.

'When the wazungu first came here, dada was very ill. So much work, and our poor dada managing it all by himself...that took its toll and he lay sleeping for some time. The wazungu saw this as a golden opportunity and, using rope ladders, scaled the mountain and reached the top.'

'He reached the peak near dada?'

'Yes, the pure and frozen peak where no mortal had set foot, the wazungu who had pierced through the seas and come to our land, gradually reached our dada himself. He took great care of dada. Lake saheb's baba told my baba that dada was very pleased with the wazungu and said to him, 'From now on, you take care of the affairs of this place. And put your benevolent hand on the head of my black people. The black man is very innocent, knows no deceit or intrigue. Today onwards, I am handing over all this land, these streams and rivers, the farms and fields to you.'

'Then what happened?' asked the hungry Darodo, pulling out a potato from the fire which was not fully cooked yet.

'What happened? What you see all around today. He started clearing the jungles. Obeying dada's orders, our forefathers began to help him. They gave up their small fields and started to work on the wazungu's big farms. Since the land had been handed over to him by dada, they also worked on it for him and survived.'

'As we are doing now?'

'Yes, but those days were not bad. Food was available in plenty, and wazungu was generous.'

'Did the wazungu give them sheep also, Mazé?' The taste of the meat of sheep was still lingering on Gachru's tongue.

'There were lots of sheep those days. They wandered around like cats and dogs, even outside the wazungu's farms.'

'But now even cats and dogs are not to be seen,' Yeloba said, once again putting his favourite cat blood to his lips.

'I am talking about the old days, Yeloba. Everything has changed now. We have to pay rent to our master for every yard our huts stand on. Even so, we have to be grateful to the wazungu. He gives shillings for our wages and then takes away samuni'.

'You know what I think, Mazé? It would have been better if dada had kept control of things with himself.'

'If he had, no? What is that old saying of our elders? Once something is actually started, it is not possible to start it again in another way.' There was Aristotle's wisdom and a note of futility in the illiterate voice of Mazé.

'Sometimes frightening whistling sounds could be heard from the top of Kilimanjaro. My baba would say to us, see, dada is howling. He cannot bear to see our plight.'

'But he has lapsed into deep silence now.'

'This is the silence of a great regret, Mendaka. He is helpless, he cannot do anything about our suffering. Look there, Mazé,' Mboya said, pointing to the snow-capped peak of Kilimanjaro, 'all that thinking has frozen the wrinkles on his face.' Then, sniffing the aroma of roasted potato, he said, 'Moanji, just take out two nice hot potatoes for me.'

'For every one shilling we get, we have to face all kinds of difficulties. We leave our children on their own at home. Rafiqui, one potato for me also.'

'Why are you getting so impatient, Dogo? Everyone will get a share.' Seeing all his friends greedily eye the potatoes he had stolen, Daroro decided that he would steal and bring them potatoes every day.

'If I could get a job for half this wage, but close to our settlement, I will take it and remain there.'

'Last year we were there, this year we are here, perhaps next year we will have to go farther away.'

'And in this way, one day we will go so far away that we won't be able to see dada's peak at all.'

'You're right. Now this distance is only going to increase. Daroro, your potatoes are delicious.'

Mboya's own hunger grew hotter, like the potato hidden in the fire.

'Mazé,' said Moanji, swallowing the burning hot potato without chewing it, 'if only each one of us owned four yards of land, we could have stayed in our basti with our families and farmed the land.' His chest started burning. Who knows whether due to the hot potato or his inflamed wishes.

'Weeping and wailing will not make somebody else's thing yours, Moanji.' Mazé Mboya's old face seemed to glow with the spirit of youth. 'You are the son of a farmer, don't you know that a man thrives only when he has endured the heat and cold of life? Keep working hard at your task.'

'But we do put our heart and soul into our work, Mazé,' Gachru couldn't help himself, 'and what is the result? Not even a roof to protect us from the bitter cold. We will spend all night shivering under the open sky.'

'When there is fire, why do you need a roof?'

'It is all very well to comfort yourself, Mazé, but having your own roof is something else.'

'Very true, Gachru. When I wake up in the morning, every joint is stiff from the frost,' Yeloba said in support of Gachru.

'I woke up in the middle of the night and, because of the frost, couldn't sleep for a long time. As I stared at the moon and stars in the sky, I thought, if only I could be up there, on some star, with my wife and children, and build myself a small hut, have a small farm of my own...'

'You have spoken my thoughts, Gachru. But now we'll have to build our homes only on the moon and the stars. There isn't even a span width of space left for us here.'

Pointing to the sky, old Mboya said in an attempt to console the men, 'These twinkling little dots are themselves homeless, poor things. They wander around all night scouring the sky to find a permanent dwelling.'

'No, Mazé. The moon and the stars are like our earth. Only much bigger.'

Mazé laughed. 'You fool, your hunger for land has blinded you. Now you even mistake the sky as the earth.

But it's not your fault. A hungry man can see nothing but a roti.'

'No, Mazé Lake saheb's clerk was telling me that the wazungu is making arrangements to reach there.'

'Arré, where all will the poor wazungu reach? Just look at our Dada Kilimu–his head rises above all the stars.'

'That's what I am saying, Mazé. If the wazungu could reach the top of dada's peak, it will not be difficult for him to get to the stars.'

'Wouldn't it be wonderful if we too could get there? We will be able to see old Dada Kilimu from up close. We will speak to him, build up his confidence, and comfort him. And seeing us happy, he will be happy, too.'

'Yes, Mendaka. Dada's heart is very heavy because of our suffering. I want that all the peaks of Kilimanjaro should echo with his guffaws once again.'

'Look there, Mazé! See who is coming…'

'It is our Karaoke. I have told him so many times to return before the night falls, but when he gets free from his work he goes and sits with – what's that clerk's name – our Wato Nyosi. And then he reads the whole newspaper before coming back.'

'He is very intelligent, Mazé. You watch, one day he will rise from being a labourer and become a clerk.'

'Jambo Karaoke,' Yeloba said when he came near.

'Jambo Yeloba. Jambo Wato.'

'Jambo.'

'Come have some roasted potatoes. They are delicious!'

'Santé, Mazé.' Taking a potato, Karaoke sat near the fire with his legs outstretched.

'I have told you so many times to come back before it gets dark, son. Times are bad. Besides, there is also the danger of flies and insects in the dark.'

'Today, the conversation with the clerk was such that I got up several times to leave, but sat down again.'

'When we left the basti, toto, our mother had said repeatedly, take care of our Karaoke, Mazé. A mother's love is blind.'

'I will definitely be back in time from tomorrow.'

'What was the conversation you had with the clerk today?' Yeloba asked Karaoke.

'You see that star over there, next to the top of our dada? The wazungu calls it the star. It is much, much bigger than our whole earth.'

'Listen to that, Mazé. I told you Lake Saheb's clerk had said the same thing to me…'

'Arré, wait till he finishes what he is saying.'

'Yes, that is what. The wazungu is going to reach there soon. All the land is lying vacant there. When wazungu gets there, we will be able to get land for a shilling or two.'

'Ah, Dogo, really? For only a shilling or two?'

'Well, it was good to hear your words, wasn't it, Mendaka? Didn't I say our Karaoke will become a clerk?'

'Yes, rafiqui. If someone from our tribe is educated, it will be a good thing.'

'Now we will all be able to buy our own land.'

'The wazungu will reach there soon.' There was a rather arrogant sense of wisdom in Karaoke's voice.

'It said in the newspaper that all that land is vacant, and anyone who wants to can buy it.'

'What's a shilling or two, Dogo? Now we will have our own land, our own fields, our own huts…'

'If the debt of two sheep is redeemed, I will take my Patia to that place, too.' Makhamba began to float in the world of stars with his Patia.

'Is this true?' All of them were wanting it to be true. 'All land there is empty, vacant.'

All eyes were fixed on that twinkling star near the top of Mount Kilimanjaro. In their thoughts, they were already on that star with their families, reaching down and greeting Dada Kilimu from there.

Seeing their laughter, it seemed as if the frozen wrinkles on Dada Kilimu's face began to melt and, once more, dada's full-throated laughter made the surrounding mountain ranges dance and rejoice.

But suddenly, mazé Mboya stood up shaking his head and, with the wisdom such as that of Aristotle, said, 'Wazangu, look. All this land before you is also lying vacant and empty as far as you can see. Now tell me, is even one span width of it yours?'

'No, it is all Lake saheb's.'

'Can Lake saheb's hands not reach that star, then?'

Translated by Keerti Ramachandra

Jambo Rafiqui

The story of this country begins with the railways. At the inception of the railways, this part of the Black Continent let out a cry like that of a new-born – one who is suddenly exposed to the unfamiliar glare of light. But then the cry of the new-born child is an indication of it being alive! That's why instead of being wary, the railway employees bent their heads to read the lines on the face of this dear child of theirs. Looking at their eyes filled with love, the little one stopped crying, began to smile and then burst out laughing.

The English priest who stood next to the railway engineer sent out a prayer to Jesus Christ, and made the sign of the Holy Cross on his chest and patted the engineer's back, 'May the Son of God shower his blessings on this beautiful child, amen.'

'Kenya!' The railway engineer kissed the shining forehead of the new-born, twirled his blond, sharp moustaches and rose to uncork the mouth of a century-old bottle of whisky from Scotland.

'Kenya!' He raised his glass of whisky and in a tone full of cheer, he said, 'Kenya!'

In response, scores of hands with whisky glasses leapt into the air. It seemed as though this auspicious moment, overcome with joy, had broken into a dance in sheer excitement.

A few yards away from their English bosses, the Indian coolies sat next to the railway line in small groups around the fires they had lit for themselves. Like their masters, they too were celebrating the occasion drinking home-brewed liquor, smoking bidis and fooling around. Perhaps their laughter belied what their eyes were seeing – the sad faces of their wives and kids, thousands of miles away. Disturbed by what they saw in their heads they drank more liquor and taking a long drag on their bidis, got lost in their thoughts of being back in Bombay. What would they buy for their people...fancy shoes Rambai would love; Jeeto will be happier with a dupatta of deeper red; and how handsome would Bashir look in his English hat!

'Bashiré!'

'Abba!'

Overcome with emotion, the father and son clasped each other in a tight embrace, immense happiness flowing out in streams of tears, fountains of joy soaking their beating hearts.

'Oyé, Shafiq, whose thoughts are you lost in?'

Lal Singh too was lifting the deep red dupatta from Jeeto's face. 'Bhai, not a minute goes by when I don't think of Jeeto. I came away just two months after our marriage.'

Sighing deeply, Lal Singh looked towards the sky full of smiling stars twinkling happily, and he wondered why everything beautiful was always far away. Then it was as though he could see his Jeeto amongst the brightest of stars, draped in the same deep red dupatta, embellished with designs woven with a golden thread.

'Oye, Jeeto, listen to me.'

'Go, go away!'

'Ha..ha..ha..' Still laughing, Lal Singh was startled to hear familiar noises around him, 'Again today?'

'Watch out Shafiq bhai, black men are headed this way... chasing a lion.' Lal Singh then turned his face towards the Indian camp and hollered loudly, 'Beware...lion...lio...'

Before he could complete the word, something heavy fell upon him from behind the bushes with the speed of lightning. Another deadly force held Shafiq in an iron-like grip. Both the lions started to bore holes in the sky with their roaring. There was utter panic all around. In the meanwhile, a group of shrieking African men appeared from nowhere and descended upon the lions with their sharp-edged spears. Within minutes, with the volley of jabs in their bodies the tormented lions broke into loud bellows while dying a slow painful death.

Raising cries of victory, the Africans dug their spears through the bodies of the animals into the ground. Once the lions went cold, the Africans were ecstatic and danced around the dead bodies in a frenzy. Drawing his last breaths, Lal Singh gazed at the brightest shining star where Jeeto was beckoning to him, wrapped in her deep red dupatta. In the few remaining breaths, groaning and teary-eyed, Shafiq was also kissing the face of his son Bashir.

The noise and commotion attracted the attention of a couple of Englishmen, who reached the spot holding their double barrel guns. The Africans cast a fleeting glance at them and continued with their celebration. The Indian coolies, who were preparing to shift Lal Singh and Shafiq to the Red Cross camp, abandoned the wounded men and stood aside with deference.

'Beautiful!' exclaimed an Englishman, impressed by the sight of the jubilant primitives dancing.

The other Englishman was thinking how pleased Lizzy would be if he were to send the hides of these lions to her in England. The third one read the mind of his mate and said, 'If one were to even touch their prey, these wretched fellows will turn into one's deadly enemy. Now see how the whole tribe will taste the raw flesh of these lions. The hides will be given to those who have played the most active role in the hunting and killing.'

'Oh, look! Two Indian coolies are lying wounded here.'

'Poor things!'

It was as though the speechless Indian coolies stood pleading fervently to their masters. They stammered, 'These two are really poor, sahebji. Please save them somehow, sahebji.'

'Take them to the Red Cross camp at once.'

As soon as they heard the orders of the white masters, the Indian coolies turned their attention to the injured men.

'Don't worry. Even if they die, their families will get a pension of ten shillings each every month.'

Then he turned to his fellowmen. 'How servile these Indian coolies are! Loyal and servile.'

'Yes. Just like my pet dog. But, in fact, their loyalty itself is a validation of the efficacy of our system. When one is dependent on a competent system, initially he may grumble and make angry noises, but eventually loyalty becomes a habit with him.'

'You are right there. I am certain that once our system starts to operate successfully here, our African friends will also give up their animal-like ways and become loyal on their own eventually.'

'Ha…ha…ha.' The face of an amused Englishman narrowly escaped the sharp edge of the spear of a dancing African, and instead of being apologetic, the man continued with his dance with a couldn't-care-less attitude.

'Bloody barbarians!' Absolutely livid, the Englishman was about to spring upon the African with his double barrel gun when his colleague quickly intervened. 'Don't be a fool, Albert. A minor slip-up on your part and we will have riots on our hands, and then after the bloodshed these men will abandon work and run away.'

Albert gnashed his teeth.

'Ronny is right, Albert. We need these men for this extremely tough mission of ours. We still have to lay hundreds of miles of railway.'

Still gnashing his teeth, Albert poised his gun as if targeting something in space, and it appeared as if his ears were yearning to hear the sound of a gunshot.

The well-mannered Indian coolies gazed at the bloodstains left by Lal Singh and Shafiq as their tears flowed silently.

Dancing joyfully and jumping around, the Africans continued their screaming and shouting, savouring the taste of the lion meat in their thoughts.

Albert continued to gnash his teeth.

'Kenya!' A short distance away swaying in the wind, European tents seemed to be crying out loudly in unsteady, happy, drunken voices, 'Kenya!'

When the railway line reached the dense forests of Voi from Mombasa, the headquarters issued an order that the line to Nairobi be completed quickly.

The treacherous, narrow winding route reached up to the height of 5,500 feet. The freely-roaming, menacing wild animals and the lurking fear of sudden attacks by the savage tribes added to the challenge. But according to the orders it was imperative that the work be completed without delay. In order to accomplish this, it was essential that more African labour be employed to assist the Indian coolies. Therefore, the officer-in-charge ordered that men from neighbouring tribes be persuaded to join the work force. Responsible African staff members were sent to the homes of the surrounding tribal areas with instructions that they should sweet talk the tribal chiefs by presenting them with English clothes and hunting knives on behalf of the brave English Saheb Bahadur. They were also to tell them that the saheb was desirous of their friendship and co-operation for the completion of the railway line.

The Saheb Bahadur's African representatives organized a grand feast for the tribal chiefs, who came clad in English clothes gifted to them by the Saheb Bahadur. They enjoyed sweet buns that accompanied roasted meat of some well-fed lambs but when that did not satisfy their large appetites, the local chiefs helped themselves to half-cooked sheep legs from the fire and started to chomp and chew the meat stuck to the bones.

'This chakula of the wazungu is delicious,' said a tribal head patting a railway employee on his back, 'and it even appears puffed up. But rafiqui, if truth be told, it doesn't fill one's belly. After wearing the wazungu's…what was it again? Yes, coat… one feels tied down. Tell the wazungu not to get upset but, truly, all these things are absolutely worthless. There is great joy in wearing loose animal skin or just to be naked. Next time, don't bother to bring this stuff, though the knives of the wazungu are excellent. Tell him he is welcome to send a hundred or more of these hunting knives.'

The tribal head sliced a whole lamb that was being grilled on a big log with the knife sent by the wazungu, then burst out into wild laughter, 'This knife is a very useful thing – so easy to hold and so sharp to chop something! Yes, rafiqui, next time be sure to bring some fifty odd knives like this one, ha…. ha…ha.'

'Sir, if you send your young men to work on the railway line, the wazungu will distribute lots of shillings to them.'

'Hee…hee…hee… Shillings? What will we do with these useless pieces of yellow metal, rafiqui?'

There are various kinds of metals scattered all over our region. Tell your wazungu to help himself to any number and any type of metal he desires. I always maintain that you black youth of today have lost your minds, that you drive yourselves so hard the whole day chasing after these worthless pieces of metal. Go inform your white men that all my young lads will present themselves early in the morning to help them. But rafiqui, we do not desire any money. If your wazungu can send knives that would be good enough and if they do not do that... even that would be fine. The wazungu are our guest, and it is our duty to come to their aid.'

'You are a very good man, baba,' said a black representative of the Saheb Bahadur, 'and our wazungu are really nice people. Let the railway line reach Nairobi, the life of the black men will transform and improve tremendously. Trains will bring novelties from far off places.'

***

Listening intently to the voice of Nature, the railway line was moving forward.

'Arré...hold on for a moment.' Nature held the hand of the railway line gently and stopped it. 'Do you see that herd of elephants? Let them go away first. These bloody animals are very cruel. If they get even a hint of your presence, they will go wild and start to trumpet in anger. They'll dig up your work and throw you into the air, smashing you into smithereens.'

'Well done! The danger is over for now and you may move forward. But do it cautiously. The route ahead goes through tricky hills…. What happened? Tired? How come? You are made of iron, aren't you? Never mind. Come, I will carry you on my shoulders.'

Riding on the shoulders of Nature, the railway line began to cover the hilly distance to Nairobi. After a while, Nature came to a sudden halt upon hearing a heart-rending scream. A cheetah had trapped an African between its sharp paws, and its teeth were digging deep into his heart, boring a hole there.

'A--aa--h!' The African who had been singing just a few moments ago collapsed and his soul ran shrieking into the dense forest.

'Bang...bang...' Two bullets fired from the rifle of the English officer silenced the blood-licking cheetah for good.

The officer got himself photographed standing next to the carcasses of the cheetah and the African. This photograph will be published in the papers. Lal Singh and Shafiq's photographs had also been printed in various newspapers and were seen by Jeeto, who then threw away her deep red dupatta; Bashir had cried till he could cry no more, and had driven himself into a state of frenzy. Looking at the soul of the dead African running through the forest, the bushes whispered to each other, 'Now who will sing to us?'

Nature gave a pat to the railway line and said, 'Don't get nervous. Let's move forward. Some sacrifice is inevitable when you take on mammoth tasks.'

The railway line placed her head on Nature's breast and sobbed her heart out. Nature comforted her, wiped her tears and then, holding her finger, it moved forward. In order to keep the railway line's spirit up, Nature narrated to her many lyrical stories of the moon and the stars but the line continued to cover the distance silently, like a petrified fairy bending her head over her grief-stricken heart. After having moved several miles forward, a range of mountains spread both its arms and blocked her path.

'Ha...ha...ha...' As though mocking the line by baring his long teeth, 'Tell me, little one, how will you proceed now?'

'Bang...bang...' The dynamite jumped up and down, and blinded the mischievous eyes of the mountain.

'Bang...bang...' The mountain's body was split apart. 'Bang...bang...' When the heart of the mountain was torn into splinters, the path emerged on its own and bowed at the feet of the railway line.

When Nature witnessed her beloved mountain blasted to tiny fragments, her voice drowned in a flood of tears, 'Poor child of mine–this mountain stood here with such pride for thousands of years. Look, despite having died, its two parts torn apart at the centre stand tall and regal. Your hard-hearted cruel men have brutally murdered my precious child. I feel like tearing them all to pieces, and then strangle you before getting rid of you.'

Nature's anger made the railway line tremble in fear.

'But no,' Nature took hold of herself and said, 'I will lend my support to you because I had promised to do that. But listen, tell your men not to be so heartless.'

After moving ahead a little, Nature leapt to stop the railway line. 'Look, this is the breeding ground of various types of deadly snakes. Look again...how they have bored holes into the earth at various places to make homes for themselves. These creatures are very treacherous. Take each step with caution... eyes alert and watchful...hold your breath.'

'Just a few more miles and we will be out of reach of these wretched creatures. Well done. Now you can speed up and reach Haathi River. Our destination is not far from here,' Nature pointed out.

At the thought of being close to the goal now, the railway line forgot her exhaustion. Tripping and stumbling, it hobbled through Haathi River to reach Nairobi amidst loud cheering. The whole of Nairobi stood there to receive her with arms wide open. People went berserk with excitement, and loud music welcomed her. Music made the railway line's heart jump with joy. The top railway officials accompanied by other honourable citizens came forward to greet her.

From a distance, Nature watched the railway line meet her people. She slunk back silently and receded far back into the dense forest.

'Kenya!' Glasses full of old brewed whisky were raised in toast.

'Kenya!' The whole country reverberated with the echo.

The railway engines, newly imported from England, started to pull luxury carriages from Mombasa to Nairobi – similar to a victory march, introducing the dark regions to the new light of modernity. Distraught by the continued sound of chug-chug and the shrill, piercing whistles, Nature receded further back into the jungle. The jungle was cleared around the railway line, dreaded animals ran off miles away and soon many small villages mushroomed there. The government appointed chiefs in these settlements and issued instructions that they take care of the problems of the black people. Indian traders set up all kinds of shops and since items of daily need could not be bought from them without cash, black settlers had no choice but to seek petty jobs under the supervision of the chiefs appointed by the wazungu.

To earn a living, some Africans became railway coolies. Some found jobs at Indian shops, others toiled as labourers in the newly set-up farms of European immigrants. Some others boarded trains to Mombasa or Nairobi, where they found jobs as peons in government offices or worked in factories owned by Ismailis and Gujaratis. There were others who found employment as houseboys in European homes, or boi(s) in Indian households, working for food and clothing, and a salary of five shillings per month. Those who found no work survived with the help of the people of their tribe as they ran around in search of work. When they got something to do, their hunger was quenched, or they were merely fed with the abuses of their likely employers.

Or they felt happy to be friends with those who had found employment. When even that did not work, they became petty thieves. A former thief who was nabbed while stealing and jailed had told them that it was fun to be in the prison of the wazungu. There you got jobs without having to run around looking for one, and the convenience of guo, chakula, and jumba came along free.

'What? Guo, chakula, and jumba free?' Those who did not succeed in getting jobs outside became eager to get arrested for some minor theft. But when they were caught stealing by the owners and were abused and kicked out instead of being handed over to the police, they were actually frustrated and envious of some lucky friend who had been put into a jail.

Gradually the phenomenon of the Indian coolies became a thing of the past. They and their sons turned successful businessmen; they became middle-rung, well-off government officers or skilled artisans. The vacancies left by Indians were swiftly filled up by Africans. Mwangi became another Lal Singh, and Matele, another Shafiq. Many Europeans became farm owners after clearing beautiful forests. And with the help of cheap African labour, they were prosperous in no time while yet others got employment as top executives in government offices.

According to official reports, the economic condition of the Colony of Kenya slowly gained strength. News of the wealth of this colony drew in many European and Asian hopefuls for work. The government proceeded to prepare many schemes in accordance with modern trends in order to ensure habitation.

More and more jungles were being wiped out. A web of railway lines and highways was spreading all around the country.

Soon, small shanty towns donned new robes and aspired to be big cities. They swaggered about in their new finery while some forests dressed themselves up as small settlements.

The god Uranus of the Black Continent gracefully accepted his defeat and handed over his crown to the beautiful god of a new civilization, Jupiter.

Eventually, scarcity of jobs in smaller settlements drove the black people to big cities in large numbers. 'When so many others have found a home there, we will also find a way to survive.' The African parts of the cities started to fill up. How was it possible to build so many schools to accommodate the children of such a large population? A lot of money had already been invested in building hospitals for the black, how could more be built? Thousands had already been given work and a few more could be accommodated, but it was not feasible to make adequate room for such a large multitude. Anyone and everyone was heading to the city.

'Black people are so uncivilized.'

'You better stay away from the black – these people are infested with dangerous diseases.'

'So many black people are sitting idle, bumming around. Why does the government not throw them into the prison?'

Many unemployed African youth would go off-track, and rolling out cigarette smoke from their nostrils, would roam the streets like habitual criminals. They moved around suspiciously, always on the lookout for an opportunity to make a quick buck. Some others would lose hope and return to their hometowns, only to come back to the city once again in search of work.

The colony continued to make progress. The new inhabitants became wealthier, and more and more Africans got employment for the completion of new projects. Large numbers of Africans kept pouring into the city, and many of them remained jobless.

Despite many schools, hospitals, and scholarships, Africans continued to be sick, uncultured, and uncouth.

This was Nairobi – the heart of East Africa. Thousands listened to its music, swaying to its magical beat, and people across Europe and Asia tapped their feet to its rhythm. A network of smooth, tarmac roads was laid out everywhere and in place of people, one could see rows of cars racing up and down. In the middle, on many crossroads sat a whole lot of manicured, green islands decked up with myriad fragrant African flowers. These islands looked like dolled-up women winking, beckoning the motorists towards themselves. On both sides of the roads are shops built in Western style with modern corridors, through which walked young women wearing skirts of the latest fashion, hand-in-hand with their beaus. They would stand in front of a shop window and whisper, 'How beautiful, darling Ledona!'

These were the corridors on which walked newly-wed, happy Asian couples – totally oblivious of the tragedy of Jeeto and Lal Singh – and they'd casually spend a thousand shillings or so on shopping.

These were the corridors swept every evening by an African sweeper who would wonder – if I were to own one of these shops, how many shillings would I possess? These many! He would pause, put his hands together to form a cup and gaze at them as though looking at a pile of shillings there – no, these many! Then he'd spread his hands apart, open his arms and ponder...and then, as if hearing the jingle of the shillings slipping from the gaps between his fingers, he would bring his hands back together and think – these many are enough.

Every year, by the side of these corridors, many skyscrapers rose high. And with contempt, they recalled the city of Nairobi as it was fifty years ago. In these skyscrapers, there is a huge number of offices – including local agencies of many international airlines where passengers from far off countries are welcomed, and air tickets worth thousands of shillings are sold to passengers who go home on vacation. There are offices of goodwill missions of foreign countries that organize conferences to discuss ways to improve the lot of African people. There are offices of import and export companies that sell meat, butter, bread and other indigenously created marvels to other countries and import motorcars, good quality ready-to-wear garments, perfumes, electric cooking ranges, and refrigerators etc.

This is the largest bank of Nairobi where hundreds of employees and clients are engaged in exchange of money. At its door, is a young man who is a matriculate standing in a dilemma, wondering whether to go in and inquire about his job application or to wait for another three or four days.

Here stands the bungalow of a very wealthy Asian, at whose gate a group of unemployed young Africans stand asking the mistress of the house, 'Mama, need a boi for the house?'

'Go, go away. There are already two such scoundrels in the house.'

Then there is this taxi driver rubbing his palms and humbly pleading to the master, 'Forgive me this one time, saheb. Please don't dismiss me. Give me one more chance.' Standing near him is his African fellowman terribly anxious with the thought that he will not get the job if the master accepts the driver's plea.

Shillings! Cents!

Hee..hee...hee... Shillings? What will we do with these useless pieces of yellow metal, rafiqui?

'We are sick.'

'Go get shillings for the treatment – this is not a charitable hospital.'

'We are starving.'

'You don't get food for free.'

'Our children are running around uselessly.'

'But where are the shillings to build more schools?'

Shillings! Cents! Nothing moves without these round pieces of yellow metal!

Nairobi!

Mombasa!

Nakuru!

The Black Continent is ablaze with lights!

When one is dependent on a competent system, in the beginning he might grumble and make angry noises, eventually loyalty becomes a habit with him.

'Why do you loiter around? If you wish to fill your belly, you have to work for it. Earn your shillings with some honest work.'

'Work? Where is work?'

'Look for work. That itself is your work.'

Two trains halted at Voi Junction between Nairobi and Mombasa. Many years ago there were unpassable dense forests here, now there are crowds of people all around. One of these trains was headed to Nairobi from Mombasa, and the other to Mombasa from Nairobi. Two black men came out of the third class coaches of both the trains. Sad and worried, they both came and stood near the water tap on the platform. They washed their faces, drank some water and then looked at each other.

'Jambo rafiqui.'

'Jambo!'

'Where are you going?'

'Nairobi.'

'Where have you come from?'

'Mombasa.'

'Here, have a cigarette, rafiqui. Why are you going there?'

'To look for work. Where are you headed, rafiqui?'

'Mombasa.'

'Where have you come from?'

'Nairobi.'

'Why are you going there, rafiqui.'

'To look for work.'

Translated by Usha Nagpal

Multiracial

The public gallery of the Parliament House was packed beyond capacity. Row upon row of black, brown, and white, African and European faces were seated on the benches. This seemed like a first-rate advertisement for the multiracial society created by a first-rate artist.

The champion of the multiracial society, Honourable Kumar, adjusted the knot of his tie with a smile. Presenting the day's motion to the House with tremendous self-confidence, he said that the government should take urgent steps to introduce the tenets of the Multiracial Society into every aspect of life in this country.

Elated, an African sitting in the first row of the public gallery raised his right arm high and inadvertently, brought his hand down to rest upon the shoulder of the Englishman seated next to him. And when the Englishman swiftly moved away in irritation, the African nearly fell on his face. His dark face tried to disguise his embarrassment with a lingering smile.

The sincerity reflected in his behaviour broadened Kumar's smile. He said, 'Our country is offering a golden opportunity. We can become the bulwark for the realization of the dreams and aspirations of the people of our community. We should take practical steps to end racial discrimination.'

A progressive English member of the Legislative Council, Honourable Light, gently nudged his companion and said, 'It is a wonder that, despite being Asian, Honourable Kumar speaks such chaste English.'

'He is the only worthy member from amongst the Asians.' Both looked at Honourable Kumar encouragingly.

'It is not a mere coincidence that our three races have come together on this Dark Continent. In fact, Nature wishes to test man's claim that his allegiance is to one race – that of humanity, and that his best virtues show up only when he extends his hand in friendship and lives amicably amongst any and all people of the world.'

'Mr Speaker and Honourable members, perhaps even the United Nations from New York will not be able to accomplish what you can achieve by the healthy growth of our Multiracial Society here. Perhaps for them, talking about mutual trust amongst nations is a mere political convenience. But for you, the subject is an everyday living reality. Now, it is up to you to either get branded as killers by strangulating this reality, or you may decide to nurture this child lovingly – like a mother does, so that the entire world becomes conscious of its strength. Gentlemen, we are mothers, and mothers do not kill their children. Rather, they bring them up by giving their own blood.'

Honourable Kumar wanted to elaborate his analogy even further but the intensity of his emotion made his throat run dry. He paused to sip some water kept on the table in front of him.

African members raised their heads to look at Honourable Kumar in appreciation and wonder, in much the same bewildered way as their primitive ancestors stood looking at the peaks of the sacred hills whispering to the sky.

'I consider it the greatest tragedy of African history that our forefathers were victims of many prejudices, and that they kept looking at each other with suspicion without any reason. Even as they lived together on the same land, they had adopted divergent lifestyles, as if they were three separate nations living on three separate continents, thousands of miles apart.'

'Honourable members, I wish to ask you a simple question. Please tell me how you would define the word "race". Although some of us with limited intelligence may be very rigid, I am sure that the progressive outlook of the majority will not be very different from my own perspective.'

Nearly all the members were happy with the thought that they were associated with Honourable Kumar's progressive group.

'The solution to this important issue lies hidden in the answer to my question. Tell me, who do we refer to when we talk of a race?'

'I have no doubts about your intelligence. Your learned looks are giving me the same answer that my own mind has given me. The idea of a race presents us with a system in which people are bound to one another politically, socially, and ideologically. Are not the African, European, and Asian people bound to each other for their welfare in this glorious country? Isn't our progress dependent on one another's? Gentlemen, I wish to pause a moment to get an answer to my question.'

As would a popular film star, Honourable Kumar looked at the spectators and raised a glass of water to his lips again to take a break. The honourable members of his group cast their eyes all around, proudly smiling as if to say, 'Behold our Asian group leader! Refute his statement, if you dare'.

Looking at the speaker, Honourable Kumar said confidently, 'My dear sir. I understand that a huge majority in the House agrees that actually it is not three different races that reside in this beautiful country. Rather, all the people are associated with only one race. We are all Africans!'

'Hear, hear!' one African member said spontaneously. Displaying his big, strong and white teeth, his shimmering dark face broke into laughter.

'Hear!' an alert Englishman too spoke up, adjusting his artificial denture firmly to give his voice some weight, 'gentlemen, ours is an African society, a multiracial society, all members of which are equally dependent on one another ideologically, socially, and politically. In the context of this reality, the principle of equality is inevitable in our culture.'

Similar smiles spread on the lips of the public sitting in the gallery. All of a sudden, an African and a French man started sneezing due to the chill in the air. The French man elegantly fished out a neatly pressed, beautiful handkerchief from his coat's upper pocket and primly covered his nose with it. The African too had a handkerchief in his inner pocket but it was dirty. He let it remain there, partly because he did not know how to use a handkerchief correctly, and partly because he was ashamed of his stinking hanky. A few small drops of water from his nose and mouth sprayed on the left cheek of an attractive Asian lady.

'Idiot,' the Asian lady thought with contempt spreading on her face, 'not an iota of good breeding in these barbarians.'

'Honourable members, we have a common culture. Why should we not then put aside our petty class differences to establish a cordial atmosphere in order to achieve a unique multiracial culture? Why should we not attempt to make this unity an enduring feature of our existence? The time has come to give up our artificial divisions and come together in our daily lives. Our children should obtain education in multiracial schools. Our lifestyle and activities should be the same so that it'd be possible for us to showcase our exemplary multiracial culture to the world by coming close to each other.'

Impressed with the speech, an old Englishman prayed to Jesus and took out a cigarette from his very expensive cigarette box. He presented it to a young Asian sitting by his side. The beautiful Asian lady also forgot about the African's sneeze and took pity on his misery. When she opened her chewing gum box, she felt like handing over the entire box to the African.

'Honourable members, before you go any further to discuss this movement of mine, I consider it my duty to caution you all that it will be suicidal to oppose this peace-oriented humanitarian motion.'

'Sirs, do you wish to commit suicide?'

Shedding aside the constricting noose of division, they began to view each other with affection, as if amongst the members of the same family. The warmth of their generous sentiment raised the temperature of the cold atmosphere.

Honourable Kumar nodded affectionately like a father watching his children playing happily with each other.

It was lunch time. Before carrying on with further discussion, the gathering broke up.

An African member of the Legislative Council shook Honourable Kumar's hand vigorously and said, 'Congratulations! I am very impressed with your speech!'

One circumspect European member said, 'Well done, Honourable Kumar. I agree with you in principle but there are a few things that do need to be discussed.'

'Kumar saheb, you spoke very well,' an Asian member said, looking at his great leader appreciatively. 'There's no time to go home for lunch now. Why don't we eat in some restaurant?'

Honourable Kumar and his companion walked a short distance from the Parliament House and halted near a bar. Stepping inside, Honourable Kumar noticed that there were only Africans sitting there.

'This appears to be an African bar. Let us go and sit in our bar,' Honourable Kumar remarked unthinkingly as he beat a hasty retreat.

Translated by Meenakshi Bharat

O This is the shape of our world. Exactly like a fat person with a bloated stomach in which the dreadful viruses of some lethal disease may be bubbling.

After having read thousands of poems in praise of God, this is in fact the first realization one gets – that our world is really one big madhouse. This madhouse is home to countless communities – the mad, the half-mad, and the sensible. The sensible ones are however, more mad than the mad ones because they actually consider themselves sensible. You know very well how these sensible communities speak at world peace conferences – in soft measured tones, about progress, peace, and friendship, and then suddenly jump to giving open threats to destroy the world with their hydrogen bombs. Just like a dangerous lunatic who, speaking with immense love and grace, will draw out a knife all of a sudden and attack you without any reason. Anyway, just as we require a few sensible people to look after a lunatic, we cannot exist in this world loaded with the mad without a few sensible communities. Even if they are sensible only in name!

0–within this egg-shaped madhouse, there is another madhouse…another world – Africa.

There was a time when, in its dense darkness, loud guffaws of wild animals and savages wandered freely, like the bubbling of unknown joys behind the closed eyes of a sleeping child.

But the dreaming child woke up bawling as soon as the sun rose and God alone knows where that carefree darkness got lost.

When the civilized races reached here, mad with hunger and sniffing for food, their torches of culture burned bright as they continued to push their way inwards into the continent, carving new roads. Horrified and surprised, the earlier laughter, reverberating without a care, stopped in its tracks as it saw the burning lines advancing towards itself. It burst out weeping. Flames rose all around them, and terrifying fires swallowed painful roars of countless animals. Hot breaths of the tormented black people filled the air. And the pretty little tweets of the baby birds lay scorched in its heat.

Lakhs of black people were brought to the shores as slaves. They were loaded on ships and transported like cattle to Europe and America in ships. On the way, some of them jumped into the ocean, and their spirits flew back home swiftly, to clasp their weeping brood to their chests.

'Mehedi.'

'Meete.'

'Zai.'

Mehedi, Meete, and Zai. Each one of those children felt that their lost fathers had returned to hold them against their chest, embrace them and kiss them all over. They were soon lost in the caresses showered on them. But in a few moments when they did not find them their love turned into bitter sobs. They would run to their heartbroken mothers then, and laying their heads on their laps, they'd cry till they slid into persistent hiccupping.

'Morons!' the cultured European would exclaim in exasperation at such scenes amongst the savages, demonstrating his total inability to feel their anguish.

'Idiots!' the savages continued to complain in their primitive tongues.

'Stupid!' How would Europeans understand these unknown languages?

At long last, after hundreds of years, the dormant conscience of European races woke up and turned its side in a hurry.

Writers have described the history and condition of black people in the following way – scores of priests and doctors, carrying loads of Bibles and boxes of medicines with them, rushed into the continent to wash clean the festering wounds of the soul and the body of the primitive natives.

But for the progress of a nation, just priests and doctors are never enough. Had the other experts and professionals not arrived here to explore the hidden wealth of Africa, this huge continent would have been snoring in its dark slumber even today. The gold mines would not have been found where thousands of African men work today, and the green flourishing farms belonging to Europeans would have remained barren and haunted. And instead of the cultured European rule, till today we would have witnessed savagery and barbarism.

It was Europeans who educated the primitive natives and turned them into human beings. If you wish to make animals your pets, you really must begin by first making them humans, teach them to clothe themselves (even though they only have rags for cover, they are certainly better off than their naked forefathers), and give them modern shelters (when the cold outside froze their bones, those huddled inside a hut in tens or twelves must thank their God for his generosity).

They made tarmac roads on which whizzed past long cars, sometimes crushing the black labourers and unemployed ruffians. But those who are familiar with the culture of such traffic do understand that such threats are from cars whose prosperous drivers are driving under the influence of alcohol, or else they are preoccupied with their beloveds.

Some strangers are bewildered that some Africans are – just like Europeans or even Asians – lawyers, doctors, or professors. And that they look exactly like them as they go about their work. But they do not realize what the earlier generations went through. If the stranger spares even a moment of thought to the struggle that several generations put in because of which the black stand where they do today, with pride, there will be no surprise then. In the last year itself, a single government trained fifteen hundred Africans as telephone operators. Even till yesterday, these people were incapable of speaking two correct words in English. But today, if you were to phone them, you would end up suffering from an inferiority complex. They sound as though they are speaking from the British Broadcasting Corporation – unbelievably refined and effortless.

Perhaps you have not had the opportunity yet to meet their women. There's a wonderful monthly magazine that is published in South Africa – *Tarram*; if you were to see black memsahebs in different poses in the magazine, you will be shocked. Even Hollywood butterflies are in a spin when they chance upon these photographs.

But there is one thing I cannot comprehend. For several years, in spite of this amazing progress, many parts of this black land have seen countless uprisings...as if all the inmates of a mental asylum have suddenly felt a wild current pass through them and they, in a united voice, are loudly raising slogans for freedom, for independence.

'Uhuru! Freedom!'

Arré, you are crazy, what freedom are you looking for? Freedom to go back to the wilderness? To remain starving and naked? Freedom to prove yourselves fools?

'Long live the revolution!'

Why do you scream so much? Why not use your newly-acquired education? Meditate in silence on the meaning of revolution…a revolution that has risen within you before you have reaped the fruits of the hard work of your benefactors.

Africa is ours!

In these times of the Sputnik, where even God's own creation does not belong to Him, who are you to make this claim? No one pays any attention to the meaningless screams of the insane. If you want further progress, then fix your unhinged minds first.

Nairobi is another madhouse inside Africa, where black Africans, white Europeans and brown Asians smile at one another because they truly hate each other. Several local agents have, in fact, printed colourful pamphlets on beautiful art paper in which you get a glimpse of the astounding progress made by this city in the last fifty years under the wings of European leadership.

Here, take a look at these pamphlets with luring pictures of American-type hotels. Rather than wandering around here and there, one can enjoy luxuries of life with a mere fifty shillings a day in any of these hotels. Here is another pamphlet that offers information on all the popular landmarks of the city. This is the City Park, where every Sunday evening groups of connoisseurs gather to enjoy bands playing English music. They take turns at playing cards, and the gossiping onlookers pause and clap loudly to encourage the musicians.

This is a picture of the National Park where elephants, lions, and rhinos roam around freely. Upon entering this park, one has to roll up all windows of the vehicle as per government directive. If you park your car close to a lion's den, they don't attack you but they sit together gossiping amongst themselves. God alone knows about what! It is as though this royal family of the forest is in prison despite being free. They say that these lions sometimes suddenly flare up, like the ones in the jungles. The game wardens then teach them a lesson by starving them for days to set them right. Ultimately, they become like helpless, weak people who recall rules one by one on their own.

This is the City Garden where trees from all over the world have been grown – trees that have spread and grown high, sucking on the fertile black soil on which they thrive like the foreigners who have descended on the city. In a corner of the garden stands an ancient tree, a native species…naked, dry, and weak. All day, it stands on one foot, brooding. At night, exactly at twelve o'clock, one can hear it sob softly. There is a popular legend amongst the black that, in fact, this is the ghost of an African boy that cries every night. This young *habshi* had committed suicide here. Once, on hearing this tale, the beautiful young wife of an English friend of mine turned her loving eyes towards her husband as if asking, 'This young African must be a dejected lover? Tell me Jimmy, had I too refused to marry you, would you have committed suicide under an old tree like this one? How wonderful Jimmy!' Then her eyes welled up, as if she was hearing a love song while gazing at the tree.

I felt sorry to crush the young lady's fantasy. 'Madam, I am afraid this story has no love and romance in it. It is a straightforward story. The African boy was actually mad. But the mad too feel hungry just as we do. One day, the starved young man ate the raw meat of a sick dog and was tormented by an unbearable stomach ache. He killed himself under this tree.'

Oh! But I was showing you the photographs of the beautiful sights of Nairobi. Take a look at this…from here starts the most popular bazaar of this city. Here, the sweet talk of the Asian shopkeepers plays on the minds of the customers. The city's four posh cinema halls are around this very market place.

Look to the left of the chowk, there in the corner is the Ismaili Community Centre, glowing with thousands of tiny lights. Sometimes, in this immense light, the Africans are able to see the dense darkness of their own lives, and they stumble and fall flat on their faces.

This is the Legislative Assembly building. It was constructed just a few years ago. On the tower clock of this building, a long, heated debate has been going on in the local newspapers recently. One group felt that the tower clock should chime on an hourly basis, while another group thought the hourly chimes would be a disturbance to their peace. Why don't you too think about this issue? I find the second group's opinion more convincing. The immense noises of the fast lifestyle of today have disturbed our balance so much already, that additional chimes will only jeopardize our lives further.

The city's Council is also very quick-footed. Within a few years, the untiring efforts of the members have totally changed the appearance of the city. Looking at the well-planned streets and lanes it would appear that a modern European city has been planted here. You feel giddy seeing the unending lines of brand new cars during lunch hours on the Princess Elizabeth Highway. The use of horse carriages has been banned for years now, since the animals would spoil the spick and span roads. This is the reason why, despite the best efforts of the City Council, some parts of the city remain filthy – where people live like animals. If, by chance, a vehicle were to pass through these streets, groups of half-naked African children would suddenly appear. Breathing whiffs of dust, they'd clap gleefully, staring at the backs of speeding cars with their grimy eyes.

No stone has been left unturned to improve the lives of the city's Africans. Education projects worth thousands of pounds are being proposed. They receive free treatment in hospitals.

Several religious missions are aided heavily by the government in order to provide enlightenment to their souls. Untold amounts of money are being spent for the African Housing Scheme. But despite such wonderful work, some egoistic, ungrateful people continue to bad mouth and sling mud on these benefactors.

'Why have these restrictions been imposed on us?'

Someone should ask them how they would ever learn social niceties if not for these harmless restrictions.

'We should have the freedom to move around freely everywhere.'

Just see, in spite of being in cities, these people still believe they are living in jungles…the poor things have not yet learnt the ways of cultured living.

'We wish to return to our old lives.'

'Mad! Absolutely mad!' Even now, they keep turning to look back at darkness.

Fifteen or twenty years ago, there was a very peaceful atmosphere around this beautiful city. European officers were very generous. Asian clerks and traders would sing praises of the government. African servants would easily accept a monthly salary of a few shillings and some leftover food that came their way. All communities loved each other, all were content and happy. But everything has changed in these last few years. There is suspicion and mistrust all around, each one is in dread of losing it all or getting it all. It seems as if all are constantly at the edge of their conscious selves and at a high alert, waiting to hear their own final screams, just before losing their sanity.

Inside this third madhouse is another strange spot, another madhouse, the Atharo Mental Hospital situated on Nairobi-Thika Road. Actually, our story begins at this point.

For the last six months, a dangerous madman is undergoing treatment in this asylum. Therefore, he has been confined to a solitary cell behind strong iron grills through which he watches the outside world each moment. His flaming eyes look everywhere as if visualizing the destruction of all he saw, and then as if he sees the whole world aflame, he bursts into loud guffaws suddenly. He grates his teeth in utter frustration of not being able to break through the grills. Standing upside down on his head, he rubs his head into the ground with devilish force as if to bore a hole into it, so that the Atharo Mental Asylum falls into deep blackness before the evening.

The other inmates stand in attention as soon as they hear his voice, as if their Lord has sent out a call. Just examine his frightening countenance, it is a replica of some blood-thirsty beast. The entire staff of this madhouse tries to stay away from him. If they could have their way, they would tie him up to the cell bars and shoot him. It is not as if the staff is not dutiful. They do feel at peace by serving these inmates in the lunatic asylum. But with Macharia, it was a different matter altogether. It's just two months since this monster killed a pious lady with terrible brutality.

Macharia was serving a sentence in the Nairobi Jail before he was declared mad. One day, he escaped from the jail. But then, how could he have evaded the law for long? He was finally caught. After this criminal act, his sentence was extended.

One day, he was breaking stones for the new exit road of the jail. Silent. Brooding. Who knows what was going on in his head? It suddenly took off on a spin. Lashed at by the warden's whip, his skin was peeling off but oblivious to everything around, he continued to count the trees of his village. He carried on talking to his wife and calling out the names of his pet sheep loudly. Eventually, when the jail monitors had beaten him blue and were exhausted, they were convinced that Inmate 115 had gone mad. They pushed him into the closed lorry of the Atharo

Mental Asylum, and laughed saying, 'Go, go, we are sending you to your woman, your wanawakhe.' After a day or two of detailed observation, the asylum doctor came to the conclusion that this inmate's madness bordered on dangerous.

Four months passed by without an untoward episode. Mrs Home of the asylum hospital behaved very affectionately with Macharia. She used to announce proudly to the doctor, 'Just wait and watch, my love will heal this unfortunate prisoner better than your medicines.'

'Do give it a try, Mrs Home, but beware, at times the madness of such patients increases manifold if they are paid too much attention.'

Mrs Home looked after Macharia very well, partly because she had begun to look upon him as a professional experiment, and also because she really was like a bowl overflowing with the milk of human kindness. She deeply sympathized with the black. Often, she would fish out her handkerchief and dab at her beautiful green eyes while talking about them, the poor dear Mrs Home.

Mrs Home had also arranged for an excellent diet for Macharia. In addition to the regular food assigned to him, she brought eggs, toast, butter, and fish from the English Mess. He would gobble everything up with relish, and then turn to stare at the smiling Mrs Home, standing on the other side of the iron bars, as if he wished to gobble her up as well. Mrs Home's smiles would suddenly shiver with some unknown dread and then, as though she recalled some task that awaited her, she'd rush back hurriedly towards her office.

'Ha, ha, ha, ha,' smelling her fear, Macharia exploded into insane laughter.

One dusky evening, as was his wont, Macharia banged hard on the grills of his cell gate. It opened. The warden had forgotten to lock it. Macharia the madman, crawled out of his cell on all fours with utmost caution of a sane being. As he headed towards the outer gate, hiding carefully from all possible eyes, he stopped in his tracks when his eyes caught sight of something shining in the corner of the corridor. The gardener's scythe. A sudden ghastly thought rose in the lunatic's head…as if the scythe, seeing itself soaked in the blood of an innocent victim, cringed in terror and pleaded to be let off. But the madman would not hear any of it.

As Macharia grabbed the scythe, he spotted Mrs Home, her back to him a little distance away. Humming happily, she was returning to her office, perhaps after having given an injection to some lunatic. She would now go back home, free from her day-long duties. She'd wash up and change into loose clean clothes, snuggle up to her husband, and share with her children the sweet little details of their school.

'Thud!' The scythe's sharp teeth sank into Mrs Home's left shoulder as if mowing through green grass, and descended into her heart where her little children were jumping up and down, clapping joyfully. And then a heart-wrenching scream! As if this was the scythe screaming, not Mrs Home.

Sons of savages! Lunatics! But Macharia's was not a fake madness. He was truly mad, totally incapable of recognizing his benefactor. Absolutely mad.

The wardens beat him up and kicked him back into his cell, and he landed flat on his face, smashing his two front teeth. In that delirious state, Macharia was walking back to his village, under the open skies, surrounded by vast dark jungles all around…treading on familiar paths, striding briskly in freedom.

Translated by Chandana Dutta

Rascal

•

Kameena

I was sitting in the car, waiting for my wife who had gone shopping in some shop nearby.

'Jambo, babu.'

I raised my head to see a well-dressed, cheerful African at the car door.

'Jambo,' I responded sourly as if saying, 'Ok, ok, what do you want?'

'How many miles does this car give per gallon?' he asked in the African tongue.

'About 36, why?' Actually, what I wanted to ask was how it concerned him whether it gave 36 or 20 per gallon!

'I like this Morris very much. Yours?'

'Did you think it was yours?' I thought, looking at him with affront.

'Nice,' he circled the car, 'really nice.'

I kept looking at him questioningly.

'Will you sell it?'

Attentive now, I sprang up from my seat and stared at him anxiously.

'Seems to be a dangerous man,' I thought, scared. I looked around for a constable. 'In a second, he'll ask for a trial run of the car and then he'll disappear – who knows where – with it.'

In the meantime, he lit an expensive cigarette and offered me one.

'No, thank you. I only smoke my own brand.'

'Will you sell? I'll give you six thousand.' Instead of asking for a test run, he immediately made an offer.

Six thousand! Last month when I had gone to ABC Motors to sell this very vehicle, they had refused to raise their offer of four thousand shillings even by a cent.

'Maybe this man is really genuine,' I reasoned, 'after all, honest and rich people can be found in all races.'

'I have a butchery in Machakos. I have two trucks and a big saloon car. But I like your small Morris Minor very much.'

My doubts receded.

'The thing is, I need to get to Machakos by this evening. I thought I might as well take a small car along.'

Hearing this, I opened the passenger door on the other side of the car and with alacrity asked him to get in and take a seat.

'In the two and half years that I've had it, this car has never given me any trouble. It has a very sound engine.'

'I had gone to the showroom of ABC Motors today, but I didn't find a single car that I liked.'

By now, I was convinced that this man was no cheat. He actually wanted to buy this car. Six thousand shillings! I thought if I could somehow hook this customer, I would make a clear profit of one thousand five hundred without much effort. To strengthen my case, I said, 'I do want to sell this car to buy a bigger one. But the problem is, it can take ten to twelve days to find a suitable vehicle. And I can't survive a moment without this car and then…'

'But, babu, you live in Nairobi. Here, every day, new models are coming in.'

I put on an expression as if to say that I was not too interested in selling my car.

'If you agree, I am even willing to give you six thousand five hundred. Do you agree?'

'I accept,' I said loudly but then, not wanting to appear too eager to sell, I assumed a casual air again.

'Hmm…hmm.'

In a little while, my wife returned. I narrated the whole story to her with great excitement. Since the African did not understand our language, we could speak openly to each other even in his presence.

When she had heard the whole story, my wife's eyes said, 'Why dilly dally. Hurry up and close the deal, and get the money.' But, unlike other Asians, she thought it wrong to take advantage of the ignorant Africans and as if to ease her conscience, she said to me, 'It is better that *you* make a deal with him, otherwise this fool of a customer will be totally duped by the shopkeepers.'

'But to take six thousand five hundred for this car is also robbery.' My conscience, which was in hibernation most of the time, seemed to wake up. 'But where else would I get this kind of price for this broken, run-down car? Of late some part or the other has been breaking down every day.

'This is rubbish. He cannot get a better car for six thousand five hundred anywhere.' My wife's passive conscience too turned a deaf ear to niggling doubts, if only to come and consort with my dormant one.

'Yes,' I had begun to think, 'ABC Motors are bloody thieves. This is a very good car. It runs perfectly on the road. And yet, they priced it at a mere four thousand five hundred!'

'Listen brother,' I turned to the African, 'even though I don't really want to sell my car, for your sake I will agree.'

The African thanked me profusely, as if I had done him a huge favour by accepting his proposition.

'Look here, you can have the car examined by a mechanic before you make the payment. Or at least you can test it yourself. It's better to be absolutely satisfied before making any deal.'

The African laughed and said, 'I have been a mechanic myself. There's no need to show it to anyone. I can gauge the right price of a vehicle as soon as I set eyes on it.'

'Even so, it was my duty to warn you,' I said gleefully. Actually, one is very happy to perform duties that have the possibility of some personal gain. In doing so, one is actually convinced of being very dutiful.

'Okay babu, since you insist, I will drive the car and see.'

As I got off the driver's seat and sat in the passenger seat, I was afraid that the test drive might scuttle a done deal.

'I have half the money with me now. But the rest is in a hotel not far from here. Let's pick up the remaining money on our way,' he said as he started the car like a seasoned mechanic.

'This one really seems to be a good man,' my wife's voice echoed from the back seat, as if she was saying, 'this man seems to be a fool; it is better to be careful, lest he take the car to a strange place and we end up paying a heavy price'. Meaning if he did not turn out to be really foolish as expected to be, all our cleverness will go for a six.

'Hmm..,' lighting a cigarette, I nodded in approval trying to look wise, 'you drive really well!'

Feeling the stickiness in my own voice, I remembered my guru who used to make ten cents on what he sold and another ten just by praising the customer!

The African looked swollen with happiness.

'My name is Arvind. What is yours?' As I spoke Swahili, I tried to mimic the tone of my African houseboy.

'Jeepu. I had a jeep I used to drive very fast. That's why my friends gave me the name Jeepu.'

Glancing at the speedometer, I stopped laughing. 'You're driving very fast. If a cop sees us, he'll issue a challan.'

'This wretched fellow has brought us into the black area,' my wife sounded frightened. 'I am wearing ten gold bangles and a necklace…hope he doesn't get into any mischief.'

I too was beginning to get scared but I pretended nonchalance and said, 'Tell me brother Jeepu, how much farther to your hotel?'

'Not too far now.' He turned into an alley where one could see only blacks all around.

'I tell you… I smell a rat here…just be careful.'

I straightened up in my seat and to bring him under control I said assertively, 'It'll be better if we finish our business quickly. I have to go pick up my pistol licence,' as I uttered the word pistol, my voice took on a rather absurd melodramatic tone.

'Yes, yes, not too far now.'

A little later, when he turned into another twisted lane, I tried to buoy up my courage and said to my wife, 'Don't worry. The guy doesn't seem to be a bad man.'

'You are an absolute simpleton. And you've turned me into a fool like yourself. If something goes wrong now, what will we do?'

'What can go wrong?' But I knew a lot could go wrong.

'No one can reason with you. You should have thought of all this before getting into the deal. No matter how much of a fool anyone may be, no one will give six thousand five hundred for a thing that is worth four thousand five hundred!'

'Why didn't *you* think of this earlier?'

'What earlier? I have simply got into the habit of quietly following you.'

In the meantime, Jeepu had come to a halt in front of a hotel. 'Be back in a moment,' he said and strode into the hotel quickly.

'Look, you need to get into the driver's seat now, keep the engine running and remain absolutely alert. If Jeepu doesn't return in five minutes, we'll go back.'

'Okay,' I said, taking my wife's advice seriously.

While the broken rattle of our old car mocked at our racing heartbeats, we sat with dazed eyes focused on our watches, waiting for something to happen, quite like the characters in a typical detective novel. Alert and on our toes, despite sitting. But nothing happened. Exactly after three and a quarter minutes, Jeepu appeared in the doorway with a bag, smiling as he slipped easily into the seat next to mine.

'All right babu, now you drive,' he gave a shake to the wads of new notes in the bag and said, 'now where do we get the form for the transfer of the car?'

'I was worrying unnecessarily. He's turned out to be a very good man,' my wife quipped. Meaning, a great fool after all!

I smiled at Jeepu and said, 'Don't worry, we can pick up the transfer form from anywhere in the big bazaar.'

As I was reversing, my wife woke up to another great danger, 'The man seems to be honest, but who knows where he's got this money from…maybe he's stolen it. Think about it.'

I was rattled, 'So, what do I do now?'

'What should one do? I am not suggesting that you go back on the deal. All I am saying is that you should manage things in such a way that we shouldn't have to face any trouble later, after the sale of the car.'

Sound advice, this.

'I'll tell you what, take him to Omi and get all the paperwork done in his presence.' Omi is my wife's brother and a barrister.

'That's a good suggestion.'

A short distance later, an African called out loudly to Jeepu from a truck.

I stopped the car.

'The truck's run out of petrol,' he told Jeepu.

'This is my truck. I bought it last year for twelve thousand.'

'Your butchery in Machakos must be huge,' said my wife, perhaps wishing if only her husband had been a butcher rather than a civil servant, he too would have been very rich.

'What's there in a salaried job!' Then she turned to me and said in our own tongue, 'We too could have been rolling in money had we started our own business rather than slogging uselessly in a government job.'

'Yes, yes. You're absolutely right. Even after crossing vast oceans to come here, if one has to fritter one's life away, it would have been better to have remained in our own country.' I genuinely felt very sorry for ourselves.

'I've told you so many times to check the petrol before starting from home,' Jeepu said to his truck driver. He turned to me and told me, 'If you have twenty five shillings, give them to this man. I only have big notes. I will return this amount along with the cost of the car.'

I put my hand in my pocket and fished out the sole twenty shilling note in it. 'I only have twenty.'

'I have a fiver,' offered my wife.

'Asante sana…thanks,' he took the twenty-five shillings and gave them to the driver. 'Make do with this.'

When I got out of that African area and turned towards River Road to go to Omi's office, many teeny-weeny thoughts were doing rock 'n' roll in my mind. 'I will buy an old car for four thousand five hundred. Of the remaining two thousand, I will get a suit made for three hundred. With about two hundred to four hundred, I will take care of the wife and kids. The rest, I'll deposit in the bank.' The digits in my bank book entered my mind and began to dance to the quick beat of the rock 'n' roll.

'Honk...honk...honk...' I barely escaped banging into a double decker bus.

'Drive carefully,' directed my wife.

'We've made a cool profit of two thousand without lifting a finger,' I thought aloud, paying no attention to what she'd said.

'You're really so naive. People make lakhs without batting an eyelid, while you're getting excited over just two thousand!'

'When we get another car, brother Jeepu, we'll come to Machakos to visit your butchery. You must be having a big business there.'

'Yes babu, Mungu has been very kind. You must come, bring ma'am along, too. I'll take you hunting.'

'These people are so hospitable,' my wife said to me, 'after wrapping up the work in Omi's office, let's take him home. Give him some tea.' I felt as though my wife was mentally busy counting the six thousand in notes of hundred. The rough lines on her face softened. Using the kitchen Swahili she'd picked up, she asked Jeepu with great warmth, 'How many children do you have?'

'Six.'

'They must be studying?' I tried to pitch in but suddenly a brown cat came running into the middle of the road.

'Ro-ra.' I swerved the car to save the cat and became breathless in the bargain.

'I told you to drive carefully.'

'What drive carefully?' I said to my wife in irritation and then cursed the city council, 'Now see, dugu... We drivers buy hundreds of licences, but look at the poor services we get!'

Jeepu nodded in agreement and lit his expensive cigarette, offering one to me. This time I did not repeat my excuse of smoking only my special brand and accepted it quickly.

'Just look at this road! Potholes everywhere and no one gives them any thought. Hundreds of stray cats and dogs jump around in the city. No one feels responsible for putting an end to the menace.'

'You are right, babu.'

'I say,' my wife said to me, looking at the huge billboard of a jewellery shop, 'we will have about one thousand left after buying another car. Get at least ten bangles made for me.'

'Babu,' Jeepu said, as if suddenly recalling something, 'could you please stop here for a minute. My cousin lives down this lane and he will be very happy to see this car.'

'Yes, yes, why not.'

As Jeepu entered the lane in which his cousin lived, my wife said, looking at his receding back, 'Seems to be a really rich guy.'

'And you think all blacks are good for nothing boi(s)?'

I extended my hand to the back and caught hold of my wife's shoulders and pressing them, pulled her a little towards myself. 'Aiii, we're in the middle of a market place....don't you feel embarrassed? She then moved closer, 'If you don't get me bangles this time too, I will never speak to you.'

'Do you think bangles are better than you for me? So much money without any effort! We will go home only after placing the order for your bangles.'

'Really?' But suddenly, as if a bee had stung her, she said 'Listen, I hope the fellow has not cheated us.'

I got out of the car and walked down the lane a little, but there was no sign of Jeepu. After three or four minutes of looking around, I was sure that he had pulled a fast one on us.

'Rascal.'

'Rascal.'

It was as if we called him a rascal first for the fact that he had cheated us of twenty five shillings, and the second time because for no reason, he had taken away our sum of two thousand shillings.

Translated by Meenakshi Bharat

Everywhere

·

Sab Jagah

The ship, panting and screaming like a dog beaten up, darted swiftly across the surface of the waters.

'Tomorrow morning, we will reach Karachi.' Sheikh Abdullah tucked a betel leaf into his mouth, trying to figure out whether he could quietly spit somewhere there itself or get up to go to the drain on the deck.

'And the day after, Bambai.' As if Pandit Karam Chand had said, 'Sheikh saheb, Uganda was a different story altogether. That was a foreign country for both of us. Now it's your Karachi, and ours – Bambai.'

'The ship is rolling too much today,' Sundar Lal's beautiful wife said, touching her heart with her hand.

'Arré, as long as the heart does not roll, the rolling of the boat is of no consequence.' He then looked at Pandit Karam Chand, as if issuing a warning, 'Don't turn your dirty eye this way Panditji, this is my bride, not a foreign country.'

'You are right.' Heerji Velji said, taking a cigarette out of a 555 pack and lighting it. 'Things go awry only when the heart rolls. If our hearts had been steady, why would we have left our homes and fled from Africa. Here, bhaiya Sundar Lal, have a cigarette.'

'Thank you, yaar,' said Sundar Lal, taking the cigarette, 'The best thing about being on board is that a thing worth one rupaiya is available for eight annas. How many packs of cigarettes have you bought?'

'Each individual can disembark with two hundred cigarettes. I have bought two hundred cigarettes in my wife's name.'

'Nothing wrong with that, Heerji. If somebody asks, you can always say she too smokes.'

In response, Heerji burst out laughing at the thought of his well brought up, upright wife smoking a cigarette.

'Hmpf...,' the upright lady shrugged disdainfully as she straightened her sari.

'This vessel is rather overloaded.'

'Yesterday I felt as if the ship was keeling over to one side,' Pandit Karam Chand started, 'and then, sinking. I got up, as if saving myself from drowning desperately.'

'Arré Pandit ji,' Heerji said, 'why are you worried? The bloody black people have been left far behind.'

'Yes Pandit ji. Now there is nothing to be afraid of. Sit by the banks of Ganga at leisure and chant the name of Lord Rama.'

'You're right, Sundar Lal. We will be able to digest the earnings from Africa only in a holy place. The rich seths of India are not fools to have filled up the whole country with temples.'

'Look, the ship is rolling again.'

'This time, the ship has brought a total of two thousand passengers.' Pandit Karam Chand swept his eyes across the cabin class deck, as if counting the passengers. 'There must be three to four hundred of us cabin-class passengers alone.'

'Yes, the welfare officer had said that the third class passengers are packed like animals in the lower deck.'

'Only two more days of hardship remain.' He lay down on the Dunlop bed in front of Sunder Lal's wife in the first class cabin. 'We'll get through it together.' She looked into her husband's eyes and smiled.

'What can the poor shipping companies do? Ever since the business of independence began, everyone is gathering his belongings and fleeing.'

'Yes, it is the baggage which has more weight. It took a full fourteen hours just to load it.' Sheikh Abdullah, swiftly chewing his paan, took a mental count of all the items in his luggage.

'The black coolies flung my sewing machine onto the ground at Mombasa port.'

'Just last November, my father had given me this machine in my dowry on our wedding,' Sundar Lal's wife said to Heerji's wife in confidence.

'What else did your father give?' Heerji's wife pulled her chair closer.

'The bloody habshis were purposely smashing our baggage. I had even complained to the white officer at the port. But who listens to us?'

'How carefully they do the loading on English ships!'

"No yaar, the damn luggage was too much. If the loading had not taken place in such a manner, the damn ship would have been delayed by another two days.'

'But why have these people carried so much stuff?'

'Everyone's carried it baba, including you and me. It's very difficult to leave one's house, dammit.'

'He kept stopping me from bringing so much,' Sundar Lal's wife told Heerji's wife, 'but I packed in everything down to the needle.'

'Even I have brought quite a bit,' Heerji's wife confided happily, as if she was speaking of some booty, 'we only had to leave one of his suits behind, that too, because it was in the laundry!'

'I thought that suits could be made any time anywhere,' Heerji reasoned, 'I had managed the tickets for the passage with a great deal of difficulty. I thought that I should make use of the damn opportunity.'

'They will get after us with a vengeance when they are in control.'

'The people who have stayed behind are in for a hard time.'

'We too, have left because we are troubled.'

''Remember Rattan Singh who lived down our street, Sheikh saheb?'

'Yes.'

'He used to return late from work every day. Many people tried to talk to him. But who does the youth listen to? The inevitable happened; one day, the blacks entered his shop. They beat him till he fell unconscious and made away with everything in the shop.'

'This is a minor incident, Pandit ji. The blacks landed in the big district bazaar in huge trucks in broad daylight and started beating everyone,' said a Parsi gentleman.

'What was the police doing?'

'They had cleaned out the whole bazaar and left even before the police could arrive! I have seen this with my own eyes, sir.'

'Forget about these robbers. Let me tell you about my African servant…what an honest looking fellow, so helpless but…'

'Actually, these people can never be honest.'

'Just listen to me, this man had been working for us for fifteen years. In our country, servants will give up their lives for their masters. In India, my grandfather had a servant…'

'Please tell us about your African servant, sir,' the Parsi said, sipping the canteen's lemonade. He made a face and set it down, 'Very stale, this soda.'

'The thing is, for fifteen years, he lived with us and kept stealing sugar. It was just by chance that I got to know of this. Otherwise, he would have kept stealing from me all his life.

I was engaged in the wholesale trade of sugar, you see. This bastard stole sugar from me for many years and ran a parallel business of his own.'

'Damn lazy bugger. My father-in-law was a rich man here. When I got married and came here for the first time, he said, 'Look son, you must be careful about two things in Africa, lumber one, the African black cobra. Lumber 2, the black man – both are very poisonous.'

'The problem is, Heerji, we cannot manage without these people.'

'Arré, you're talking of managing, Sundar Lal. You just want to say that you need the black boy for household work, isn't it? In India, the womenfolk do all the kitchen work on their own. Then why do our bloody women start behaving like memsahebs in Africa? Tell me.'

'What can I say? It doesn't matter now. We are leaving Africa for our own country. We'll have to do all our work ourselves.'

'Better to work hard with our own hands. At least we won't live with fear filled in our chests all the time.'

'Yes, brother. This kind of life is just not worth it. You may put any number of locks on your door but all the time there's a feeling that a black robber will somehow sneak in any moment.'

Sheikh Abdullah stopped speaking suddenly. A short distance away, a black servant with a roll of rope hanging on his shoulder came walking with a swagger towards them. 'Arré, this black fellow has landed here also!'

All of them turned their faces to the African.

'Seems to be crew-man.'

'But this company is Hindostanee. What business do the blacks have here?'

'This man must have surely travelled to many ports in the ship.'

'The blacks are no longer like the old blacks. I had an African cook who had been posted in the British Army in London for five years.'

'Nowadays these black people are spread all over the world.' The speaker was lying on an easy chair a yard or two away.

The African sailor came nearer and greeted them cheerfully – 'Jambo'.

'By saluting us, he is actually making fun of us,' said Sheikh Abdullah when he had gone ahead.

'He is the lone African on the whole ship. But see how cocky he is!'

'If one of our brothers were now forced to travel alone with fifteen Africans, he would die of fright.'

'A poor man only dies of hunger,' the man on the armchair interrupted again.'

An old passenger with ascetic-like appearance, walking past them on the deck, stopped suddenly as if jolted to a stop. 'That is incorrect son. The breath dries up only when a man is unable to utter the name of God.'

'Ah ha-ha-ha,' Pandit Karam Chand straightened his turban and looked at the ascetic with admiration. 'You have such great thoughts sir. Come, please take a seat.'

The ascetic sat down in a vacant armchair nearby. 'This is Shri Ganpat Rai Ganesh Dasji,' Heerji said in introduction, 'he had come to Africa from India on a religious tour.'

'He sings beautifully and does wonderful keertan,' Heerji's wife told Sundar Lal's wife, 'he had visited our town.'

'Where were you hiding for so long on the ship, maharaj?' Pandit Karam Chand asked Shri Ganpat Rai Ganesh Das, 'if we'd met earlier, we would have spent the whole journey singing the praise of God.'

'Maharaj, please sing something.' Ever since he got married, Sundar Lal had started enjoying music.

'Yes maharaj, let's have some singing,' Pandit Karam Chand also pleaded.

'Okay, son.' Shri Ganpat was coming straight from the ship's bar, which is why his face glowed like that of a mahatma. 'Go bring the dholak from cabin number 15.'

'Should I get you some beer too maharaj?' Heerji asked with apparent hesitation.

'Yes, son. The emptiness in a devotee's voice is infused with devotion and love upon tasting ambrosia.'

Within a short time after the start of the keertan, a crowd of devotees had gathered.

Radheshyam
Jai bhagwan
Jai bhagwan
Radheshyam

The drum was resounding, people were clapping, and mouths chanting.

Radheshyam
Glory be to God

That African seaman, returning from work, was looking at the faces of the chanters in awe. His lips too started moving with those of the devotees as if he too wanted to sing.

Radheshyam
Jai Bhagwan

But he could not sing. The only music he knew was the rhythm of work. All his life he had sung not a single song – not of God, not of Radhe. His lips were only used to quivering with hunger and thirst after intense hard labour. Even so, now his lips moved to the beat of the music.

Radheshyam
Jai Bhagwan

It was as if the name of God had softened his barbaric demeanour. He had started looking like a very good and gentle man.

'Arré, what is this black man doing here?'

In this cool, sweet atmosphere descended a kind of bitter, sour taste. 'Arré, this black man…'

Seeing so many eyes turned on him, the African became restless. The music became discordant. The African realized that it was getting past his dinner time and if he continued standing there, the ship's mess would shut down. As he wheeled around, he bumped into a woman.

'Hai,' the woman reacted as if a black man had leapt at her in Africa to snatch her bangles.

'He works on the ship. We've not been able to get rid of the blasted fellows even here,' another woman said, glaring at the African.

'Here you are, maharaj,' Heerji said to Ganpat ji, 'moisten your lips with beer. Your throat must be parched with the singing.'

'Yes baba, I am very hungry, too. Go get some food for me.'

Radheshyam
Jai Bhagwan

The chanting continued all night. But when daylight broke, all the passengers were talking about Karachi.

Sheikh Abdullah got all set and ready and knocked on Pandit Karam Chand's cabin door, 'Arré o Pandit ji, come. Let's go to the deck. The Karachi harbour is in sight.'

'Okay, so there you are, finally there's your Karachi,' Pandit Karam Chand said as he opened the door.

'Don't worry, soon you'll be in your Bombay too,' Sheikh Abdullah's voice was quivering with happiness.

'Pandit ji,' as he saw the lights of Karachi from the deck, Sheikh Abdullah's mind lit up with the memory of his past, 'thirty years ago, when I first left Karachi for Africa, my heart was sinking…as if I was leaving my own people weeping and crying on the banks while I dived into the ocean. Subsequently, I returned twice or thrice to Karachi. Each time, I had to toughen my nerves to return to Africa.'

'It's very strange Sheikh saheb, we think of "kala pani" as a noose and yet, we willingly embrace exile for the sake of livelihood.'

'I lived a whole thirty years in Africa but never once, on any day, did I feel it was my land.'

'How can one ever feel at home in a place where one is constantly afraid of being robbed or attacked? How can one ever feel happy?'

'Many of our Indian and Pakistani brothers are poorer than the Africans. Yet, how honourable they remain!'

'Honour is something that one inherits from one's ancestors. What honour can you expect from animals who do not even know what family they belong to?'

'Absolutely correct,' said a middle-aged man, 'I have worked all my life in the police. I had to hobnob with these people all the time. All of them are loafers. Many of them do not even know the name of their fathers.'

'Thank God, we are free of these people. Now we can spend our days happily with our brothers.'

'Our own people are solid gold, Pandit ji.'

'Absolutely correct, we have our own beliefs, our own ethics. What harm can a God-fearing man do?'

'Look, there's our custom office, over there.'

'I hope you don't have any objectionable items with you.'

'I have everything, Pandit ji. After all, we have come here to set up home.'

'I suggest that you settle the matter quietly. At the Bombay customs, this is what I always do. Even if one has to shell out twenty or twenty five rupees, at least it takes us easily through customs.'

'Thank your stars, saheb,' the retired police officer was standing in a group nearby, 'that you were successful in getting your luggage. I spent all my life in the police force there and...'

'Eighteen, nineteen, twenty,' Sheikh Abdullah took mental count of the items in his luggage and then said to Pandit Karam Chand, 'Pandit ji, when I started out with so much luggage, I thought that the blacks would make off with all of it before I could reach the ship. I have brought each item at great risk.'

'Thanks to our Lord Krishna, Sheikh saheb, there's nothing to be scared of now.'

'True, what is there to be scared of now? We've after all come back home.'

In a little while, everyone seemed to have got ready and could be seen pacing here and there. Many stood at the railings, looking out to the teeming crowds at the harbour. The passengers alighting at Karachi were restless to be done with the medical and immigration formalities. Finally, two pilot boats arrived and tugged the ship into the harbour. The rising sun seemed to say to the passengers, 'Arré, I am the same sun that you saw in Africa. I am the same all over the world.' But no one paid any heed to the sun.

Now, this morning, this Karachi, our motherland, one's own people...

'Look, there's your maamu,' a mother pointed out her brother to the child in her arms from the deck.

'That's my brother, bhai jaan.'

'My friend! Oye, brother!'

A clamour rose on the ship above and in the harbour below. The African sailor was nowhere to be seen. Wonder where he was hiding?

'Abba, I want to go home,' Sheikh Abdullah's young son insisted innocently, clutching at his father's legs.

'Arré son, we have come home.'

'No, abba, I want to go to Meetu's house.'

'Meetu was our African servant,' Sheikh Abdullah told Pandit Karam Chand by way of explanation.

'No, abba, I want to go to Meetu,' Sheikh's son was beginning to cry.

'He's only a child. Make him settle down, he will.'

'Pandit ji,' Sheikh Abdullah peered into his spectacles and said, 'it seems as if my brother has not come to receive me. I can't see any known face here.'

'Everyone is a stranger to me Sheikh saheb. Maybe I'll see someone I know at Bombay harbour.'

'Strange! Hundreds of people but can't see my brother anywhere.'

'Let it not be your brother, they are all like your brothers.' Pandit Karam Chand was perhaps thinking of his own brother who had not written to him for the past one year.

'Truth to say, strangers are sometimes better than one's own brothers!'

The ship was to leave for Bombay the next day. Pandit Karam Chand got off the ship with the purser's permission to spend a few hours roaming the city of Karachi.

'Come Sheikh saheb, let's see your Karachi.'

'Come Pandit ji, this will be a memorable experience. Come behold the delicate beauty of Karachi – even a look can soil her.'

'If you see our Bombay, your heart will come alive, Sheikh saheb.'

'Forget that old woman, Pandit ji. That poor lady has but false airs.'

'My heart is at peace after ages,' Sheikh Abdullah said after clearing the customs. His eyes swept around the scene.

'See, how relaxing it is here. Not a single African in sight. There is no question of looting and cheating here.'

Sheikh Abdullah started counting the items of his luggage; first his own, then those of his family members.

'Begum, you mind the children,' he said to his wife, 'and I'll take care of the luggage.'

'Take it easy, Sheikh saheb,' Pandit Karam Chand assured him, 'there's nothing to be afraid of here.'

But when Pandit Karam Chand returned to the ship after three hours, he looked very perturbed.

'This is the limit,' he told his friends. 'Sheikh saheb had only gone into the hotel for just two minutes, when the tongawallah made away with the trunk with all his jewellery.'

'Really?'

'This is rather strange!' Heerji's black shadow looked like that of an African watching over him, 'See, here too the bloody African…here also, the black thieves!'

'Yes, bhai Heerji. Here too is the mess created by the hungry and the poor.'

Meanwhile, the African crew-man of the ship materialized on the deck from somewhere.

'We fled for nothing,' said a passenger, 'the black man is present everywhere.'

Translated by Meenakshi Bharat

Cast in the Same Mould

•

Ek hee Roop

'Jemu!' Blind Kango left his typewriter and slid close to Jemu. 'Yes?'

'I wonder what your face looks like. You must be wondering the same about me.'

'You are truly blind, Kango.' Blind Jemu too gave up her knitting, felt around for Kango's hand and then held it in hers.

'That's how it is, my dear granny!'

'Oh, I know that, you fool, but the way you talk makes me suspect that you have lost your inner vision too.'

'What good is the inner vision when I wish to see your face? I am blind by birth but in my mind, I keep on drawing faces.' Kango began to feel Jemu's face with his other hand, 'yesterday I drew a face, Jemu – your face.'

'But you have never seen a human face…then how did you draw mine?' Jemu rested her face on Kango's shoulder.

'By probing your face with my fingers. I even showed that face to Mummy Fisher.'

'And what did she say?'

'She laughed and told me that the face I drew looked exactly like yours, Jemu.'

'Kango.'

'Yes?'

'I have never had the desire to see your face.'

'Even so, one does think about it.'

'No, I never do. I love Mummy a lot but I have never hung her picture in my mind.'

'The things you say!'

'You don't understand, stupid. Love is not dependent on any kind of face because every face of love is endearing.'

'Wonderful, Jemu!' God knows from where Mummy Fisher suddenly appeared there.

'Your words are even more beautiful than your face.'

Kango hurried to attend to his typewriter and Jemu too getting red in the face, found her fingers starting to knit the sweater fast.

'I should not have come in unannounced, children, but sometimes when a mother is overcome with love for her child, she disturbs his sleep by kissing him over and over.'

'No, Mummy. When the child opens his eyes he is happy to see his mother's face even more than a fairy's.'

'You really say the prettiest things, my child.' Mummy kissed Jemu's forehead with utmost love.

'Jemu only knows how to talk, Mummy.' Kango was now typing really fast, 'I am the one who slogs the whole day.'

Mummy Fisher stood behind Kango and ran her fingers through his hair. 'What are you typing, son?'

'You read it yourself, Mummy... I am blind.'

'No son, you are not blind... I am your eyes. My eyes are the eyes of all of you.'

'I was typing a story, Mummy. Do read it aloud,' Kango said, handing over a typed page to Mummy.

Mummy Fisher began to read it.

'We are all blind but in our previous birth we were not so. Once, we happened to see a pair of beautiful eyes and we prayed to God to bless us with similar eyes next time.

'God did accept our prayers, but how was it possible to give those two eyes to so many of us who were praying to him? He mulled over the matter but found no solution. Finally, the angels hit upon an idea. Following their suggestion, God made us all blind and blessed us with the two pretty eyes of Mummy Fisher.

May God always keep these eyes blessed and healthy.'

The story made Mummy Fisher's blue eyes moist like the blue sky when it is damp with the dense clouds. From the depth of her heart, she sent out a fervent prayer… 'Oh God, let these eyes always loyally serve and be there for these blind children.'

'Why are you quiet, Mummy?'

'You have written a lovely story, son. One day you will be a great storywriter of your country.'

'Really, Mummy?'

'Yes, son. God is never unjust to anyone. When He deprives you of one thing, He returns it fourfold with something else.'

'But Jemu thinks I am crazy.'

'But of course, you are crazy,' said Mummy, tweaking his nose, 'why Jemu, you do like the madness of this son of mine, don't you?'

'You are very naughty, Mummy.' Jemu shyly hid her face in the red wool of her knitting and burst into laughter.

'Paradise Florists have sent a huge order for baskets. I better go and attend to it.'

When Mummy Fisher left, Kango said, 'Mummy is so sweet.'

'Yes, Mummy Fisher is very sweet.'

***

When Mummy Fisher entered the basket room, the room itself seemed to hum 'Mu-mm-my'.

'Elfie, has the work for the Paradise order been completed?'

'We will not leave today till we finish it, Mummy.'

'Just one hour to finish, Mummy,' Lemba's fingers were racing on her work. Looking at the youthful enthusiasm of the old man, it occurred to Mummy Fisher that as long as there is a desire to live, one would never grow old. Age is really nothing, it is only a state of mind.

'I hope your cold is better now, son.' Lemba must have been about twenty odd years older than Mummy but while talking to him, Mummy always felt as though he was her youngest child. One way of keeping human relationships pleasant is by not basing them on ancestry and family trees but to build them upon the emotional bonds that we actually feel for each other.

'I am absolutely fine, Mummy,' the old man seemed to be saying, 'Mummy, in the lap of your maternal love and care there is no old age, no blindness, no sickness – there is nothing but joy.'

All the inmates of Mummy Fisher's Blind House were happily occupied in their assigned chores and baskets. Their joyful efforts and work touched Mummy Fisher's soul and smiling, she reassured herself – the hands of my blind children are not blind...they can see and they can work, too. There is magic in their work and that's why their feeling of helplessness has fled into oblivion. They are not able to see human requirements but because they are able to feel them, their talent to capture them is extraordinary. Given the right encouragement, they could be experts in creating even prettier artefacts.

***

Young Jackie was humming a tune while weaving a beautiful basket as Mummy Fisher watched, fixing her gaze on her slim, deftly-moving fingers.

'Mummy,' God knows how Jackie sensed that Mummy Fisher was looking at her, 'how does my basket look?'

'It's very pretty, my child.'

'Mummy, when this basket is filled with flowers and carried by a charming bellé, then dolled up with the blossoms, my hard work will appear even more fetching.'

When Mummy Fisher walked out into the corridor she saw a blind girl peeling potatoes. 'Hello, Kaniyo, peeling potatoes?'

'Yes, Mummy.'

Mummy Fisher also sat down with her for a while.

'Kaniyo, there was a letter from your father. He wants to get you married.'

Once the dark skin of the potato was removed, its white, spotless inside seemed to break into a smile.

'If you get married and go away, who will make finger chips for your old Mummy?'

'Mummy.'

'Yes?'

'Please tell my father properly what sort of groom to find for me.'

'I will choose your groom myself, child.'

'There is a custom in our tribe that the day before the engagement, the would-be groom goes and hides himself in a jungle and the prospective bride goes searching for him. Just now, I too had gone far out looking for my shepherd and had found him. He asked me, "Hey, Kaniyo, your eyes are shut, then how did you manage to find me?" I opened my palms, extended them to him and said – Look here I have my white Mummy's eyes and I always carry them with me and go wherever I please.'

'I will look for a very handsome prince for you.' On an impulse, white Mummy kissed that roly-poly potato along with its dark skin.

When she reached her office, Mummy found Miss Wadle, her assistant, typing correspondence pertaining to the Blind House. 'Good morning, Wadle.'

'Good morning Mummy. You better change this typewriter, Mummy, it has grown very old now.'

'Wadle,' said Mummy, sitting in her chair, 'this typewriter is not ready to retire just yet, and it is not nice to lay someone off against their wish.'

'But it is really ancient now.'

'Just pay attention to its sound. Despite old age, its khat-khat is so musical. Like me, this typewriter too has been serving this blind world for a very long time and it understands all its problems.' Looking away from the typewriter, Mummy was lost in a maze of memories that unfolded in her mind. 'Wadle, often when I sit down to type, I get the feeling that the typewriter is doing all the thinking and is forming words on its own. In difficult times, its ingenuity has always served me well.'

For a while, Mummy was silently occupied in systematically gathering her scattered memories, 'No, Wadle. Let this old companion of mine remain in its position.'

Wadle passed on a typed letter to Mummy for her signatures and setting her reading glasses in place, Mummy got busy attending to the official business of the Blind House.

'Mummy,' after some time Miss Wadle lifted her head and said, 'the black people are creating a lot of noise that we – all the people of the white race – should pack up and leave.'

'We have nothing to do with politics, Wadle. Our job is to discharge our duties.'

'But Mummy, the situation is getting worse. Miss Eden was telling me that this time she has no intention of coming back from Belgium once her home-leave is over.'

'That's dereliction of duty, Wadle. Just for a moment, imagine if both of us go away…who will look after these blind black people? They really need our guidance.'

'That is very true, Mummy. But the black people hate us and we cannot serve them without their consent.'

'My child, if the desire to serve is genuine, God would never close His doors for him. Have faith in God.' This was as though Mummy Fisher was trying to steady her assistant's wavering belief.

Miss Wadle seemed very impressed. Perhaps she was making up her mind to make Mummy her ideal, and spend the rest of her life serving this African Blind House.

***

'Jemu.'

'Yes, Kango.'

'Before breaking free from his shackles, one is greatly troubled.'

'That's right.'

'What I am trying to say is that our country has been kept tight in chains for so long that now after independence too, every part of her body is aching.'

'Yes, Kango.'

'And now we are in dire need of countless women like Mummy Fisher who can nurse and tend to the wounded body of our country.'

'Kango.'

'Yes?'

'My brother told me that Mummy's life is in danger. Our people don't want to see a single white person in this country.'

'No!' The sudden jerk of Kango's hand made his typewriter nearly fall off the table.

'This cannot be. No power on earth can separate Mummy from us.'

'All the foreigners are fleeing from this country rapidly. I believe, if Mummy leaves then…'

'Then, Jemu, I will make the eyes of my mind go blind, too.'

'Our race hates the colour of Mummy's skin. If she were to be black like us, our people would have worshipped her.'

'No, stupid. It was you who told me that Mummy has no colour.'

'That's just blind people's talk. Those with eyes don't see anything beyond colour and beauty.'

'Mummy is feeling very flustered. While talking to her today, I wanted to put my head on her chest and cry.'

'Yes, Kango. Mummy appears quite lost these days.'

'All the white people of the city have left. What if Mummy decides to go away?'

'Then I will truly go blind, Kango.'

'But Mummy will never go from here.'

'Yes, Kango. Mummy shouldn't go away.'

***

'Wadle,' Mummy Fisher was terribly perturbed.

'Mummy?' Miss Wadle was totally composed.

'Father Gareth had transported stones on his own shoulders while getting this church constructed.'

'Yes, I know Mummy.'

'And he wanted his grave here in this churchyard.'

'Father truly loved this church.'

'Then why did he leave, Wadle?'

Wadle bent her head thoughtfully.

'It's true everyone went away…but why these people,

Wadle? Why Father Gareth, Dr Pattison? They had made their homes here.'

'Mummy, even if we leave, we will actually remain here. These churches, schools, and hospitals are our identity; they are symbols of our souls. We will always be present here.' Miss Wadle seemed to be voicing Mummy's thoughts.

'But my resolve is weakening. I'm very disturbed.'

'Don't lose heart, Mummy. Time can never stand still. These troubled times will also pass.'

'Why did these people go away? Till they were here, I felt reassured. But now my heart is sinking.'

Alarmed, Miss Wadle gazed at Mummy's face.

'Mummy, a few months back when I wanted to run away from here, it was you who made me stay back and be at peace. In fact, I was amazed at myself. But now I am surprised to see you so distressed.'

'My heart cries out since I do not wish to desert my Blind House.'

'Then don't leave. Why do you even think about doing so? Both of us will continue to work as usual. In these changed circumstances, our mission need not change.'

'I received another threat in the morning.' Mummy was avoiding meeting Miss Wadle's eyes. 'These people want us to leave at once.'

'Who cares about what they want.'

'Brown received similar threats…and later, they butchered his whole family.'

'You should inform the police, Mummy.'

'A couple of policemen are always on guard here but when these people attack, the police are helpless.'

'Then seek Captain Robert's help. I believe his contingent is still here.'

'Captain Robert too is going back after the European evacuation. He told me that if we do not wish to leave, he is not in a position to help us. I am really worried, Wadle. Even if a few others had stayed back, we would not have faced such a difficult situation. I now feel that stopping you from going was a mistake on my part.'

'No, Mummy. You actually supported my faltering self. Now I am standing firm on my feet.'

'But my own faith is now shaky, Wadle.'

'Mummy?' Miss Wadle felt as if the very foundation of the Blind House was shaking.

'Also, Gilly has written from Belgium to say that if I don't reach him soon, he will come down himself to fetch me,'

Miss Wadle gazed at Mummy's face, 'Is this the same Mummy?'

'We will have to find a way out immediately. Father Gareth used to say that when a storm is brewing, one should shut the windows.'

Miss Wadle opened the windows of her heart and wondered why Mummy's tone was so apologetic. This was not Mummy speaking, this was someone else. People do change and their mental state does not remain the same always. But not Mummy. She never changes. Mummy is not just a person, she is virtue itself and that never changes – never!

'Dear child, Captain Robert is coming here this evening. He wants to ask us one last time if we're going to leave or not.'

Wadle was searching for Mummy in Mummy's face.

'Perhaps it is God's will that we go away. You better think seriously before the Captain arrives. I am not able to think.'

While washing the face of an unattractive blind African child, Miss Wadle seemed to be peering into his innocent mind as though responding to the call of a maternal instinct that knocked at her inexperienced heart.

All children, white or black, are beautiful thanks to their innocence. Our children are the common heritage of humanity. They have no race or creed because they have no knowledge of these barriers.

Miss Wadle wanted to run and hold the tiny fingers of all the children of the world, and become Mummy. Impulsively, she turned and kissed the dirty face of the African child. All of a sudden her face was clouded by wrinkles of deep worry. 'If we go away from here, this blind family of ours will suffer a big shock.'

'M..mummy!' the black child seemed to call out to her from his innermost being.

Miss Wadle clasped the child to her bosom.

'I am not going and if Mummy decides to leave, I will become Mummy.'

Miss Wadle started to run her fingers through the hair on her right temple exactly like Mummy Fisher did.

'But if Mummy goes all the inmates of the Blind House will go mad. They will refuse to call me Mummy. How can I take Mummy's place?'

When staring at the wall of the Blind House, Miss Wadle's eyes dug into it and her blind worry swinging on a delicate branch of her mind answered, 'Love is not contingent on a face, since every face of love is endearing.'

Translated by Usha Nagpal

Jambo, Joginder Paul!

Devendra Satyarthy

Jambo in the African language, Swahili, means salaam or salute. And I say, Jambo Joginder Paul. After all, what else can one writer say on meeting a fellow traveller?

In a somewhat similar manner, about this time last year in Karachi, Qurratulain Haider had greeted me. Haider is Annie to people who know her closely. Her novel *Aag ka Dariya* had just been published. Annie autographed my copy – 'For Devendra Satyarthy, who is amongst such people who make it possible to hope that even in today's terrible times, the tradition of brotherhood in Urdu culture is alive and will continue to be so.' I could say exactly the same about Joginder Paul because the African who breathes in his stories seems very close to me despite being thousands of miles away. Now I wish to say to Joginder Paul what I had said to Annie earlier. Paul has lived in Nairobi for twelve years. He said one day, when it's fourteen years, I'll return from Africa and then, mind you, I intend to write a whole novel on this vanvas of mine.' I shall say then, it is me who has written this novel, though it carries the name of Joginder Paul.'

When Joginder Paul read out his short story "Dharti ka Kaal" ("Land Lust") for a writers group in Delhi, each one hearing the story felt transported to Africa. I couldn't help but say, 'I am Dada Kilimu, and the frozen wrinkles on his forehead are mine too.' The same can be said about most of the stories in this volume. In the society that we are living in today, there is more and more space for voices from different countries. It is as if the whole world is one city, and the writer is like a housemaid who is privy to every story unfolding in each of the households.

I remember an African doll which my cousins from Africa had brought for me. The doll wasn't pretty but his features are etched in my heart even today. A statue of an African girl that still stands on my bookshelf, mirrors the sadness of that African doll, the one I couldn't keep with care. Later, I met an African girl who was brought up in Baroda and educated in Kanhaiya College. This happened more than twenty years ago. I do not know where that African girl is now, but when Joginder Paul read out his short story "Ek hee Roop" ("Cast in the Same Mould") in the voice of his blind African female protagonist, not only did I hear my African doll but also the echoes of the girl who had said she wanted to serve her country. In this story, Joginder Paul brings this voice to our ears through the brilliance of his craft.

'Love is not dependent on its appearance, because it is lovable no matter in what form.' In this story, Mummy is a mother who serves her blind children not as an ordinary human being but as compassion incarnate.

In the story "Jambo Rafiqui", Joginder Paul tells us how modern civilization has snatched away the native elemental nature of children of the black soil without giving them anything in return. The Voi Railway Junction is actually a symbol of African displacement and its bewildering poverty, where the only thing two Africans can say to each other is 'Jambo Rafiqui'. This moment in their conversation is a big challenge for our civilization today.

The poise that one sees in Joginder Paul's stories is an extension of the poise within him. It brings a new light with it. As the tradition goes, the images of angels do not have colour, they emanate light all around. But Paul is not miserly with his colours. The colours of his stories steal into our minds unnoticed; his characters etch out their shapes in our imagination, each marking a distinct identity.

Last year at a symposium on the 'Short Story in Urdu' in Lahore, I had said, 'Look here gentlemen, here in your land, I am willing to be the son of the short story writer yet to be born; I am not old, I am willing to walk step-in-step with the younger generation, so that I can read newer Gadariyas and meet newer Ashfaque Ahmads…' I am indeed fortunate that today I walk joyfully in step with many young writers, amongst whom is the wonderful writer Joginder Paul.

But Joginder Paul does not set up guards on the voice of truth. To understand this you must read his story Mojaza (Miracle). This is the story of that African lake on which the land beneath the feet quivers because the lake's waters are really beneath the ground, not above. You will then experience how, beneath a land of lies, shivers the world of truths.

"Har Jagah" ("Everywhere") is a story in which there is a fast-paced depiction of a people and conditions where Joginder Paul has whipped alive a biting story about the world of crime for us. In the story "Sab ka Sawal" ("Everyone's Dilemma"), Makoji is a character who goes to the courts of God after his death, to cross-examine the Divine. Similarly, "Manda" ("The Slump") is a great story in which while the rich and the famous sit sipping their drinks over so-called intellectual discussions in a club, we hear the conversation of African waiters who collect the leftovers from the glasses of their patrons to have a heady cocktail. The central character of the story sits crouched insect-like, deep in the folds of rose petals, awaiting the break of a new dawn.

It would be wrong to say that there is a lull today in the Urdu short story. I say to Joginder Paul, my dear, don't pay heed to what these people say. Theirs is the voice of those who are not able to support creativity.

Joginder Paul's book of stories, *Dharti ka Kaal*, will now stand on my bookshelf that has the statue of the African girl on it. I will read this book over and over again, and will recommend that all my friends do so as well, so that they too can witness how beautifully some Urdu short stories have built a bridge with Africa, a land thousands of miles away. Jambo, Joginder Paul!

16 March, 1961
Translated by Chandana Dutta

Glossary

Swahili

asante – thank you

boi – houseboy

bwana – master

chakola – food

dogo – small

dugu - sibling

guo – clothes

habshis – derogatory way of referring to black people

jambo – greeting

jumba – house

kuba – big

menhe – sound sheep make

mungu – god

posho – meal of maize flour

rafiqui – friend

saana – very

samuni – quarter of a shilling

sante – cheers

shembe – lion's cub

toto - child

wanawakhe – woman

wazungu – white people

Urdu/Hindi

annas – Indian currency (cents/pennies)

baba – old man, or used as an affectionate term for children

basti – slum-like settlement

beta – son

beti – daughter

bhai jaan – brother (jaan is an Urdu suffix, meaning as dear as life)

bhaiya – brother (older brother; respectful term)

bidis – local, inexpensive Indian cigarettes

chaat – savoury Indian snack

chowk – crossroads

dada – grandfather

dholak – double-ended drum

dupatta – stole long scarf

Hindostanee – Hindustani (Indian)

ji – suffix used to denote respect

keertan – religious gathering for singing devotional songs

maamu – maternal uncle

maharaj – king (also used to show great respect to someone)

mahatma – great soul

maund – unit of measurement

paan – betel leaf with condiments

Radhe – Lord Krishna's consort

rupaiya – rupee (Indian currency)

seth – merchant, prosperous person

shabash – welldone

vanvaas – exile in forest

Other Works by Joginder Paul

Collections of Short Stories
1. *Dharti Ka Kaal,* Hali Publishing House, Delhi, 1961
2. *Mein Kiyun Sochun,* Adabistan Urdu, Amritsar, 1962
3. *Rasa'i,* Nusrat Publishers, Lucknow, 1968
4. *Matti Ka Idraak,* Lajpatrai & Sons, Delhi, 1970
5. *Laikin,* Urdu Publishers, Lucknow, 1977
6. *Be-Muhavara,* Kailash Publications, Aurangabad, 1978
7. *Be-Irada,* Zam Zam Book Trust, Delhi, 1981
8. *Joginder Paul ke Muntkhib Afsane,* Seemant Prakashan, Delhi, 1987 (Pakistan Edition, 1989)
9. *Khula ,* Modern Publishing House, Delhi, 1989
10. *Khodu Baba ka Maqbara,* Modern Publishing House, Delhi, 1994
11. *Joginder Paul ke Afsanon ka Intekhab,* Taqhleeqkar Publishers, Delhi, 1996
12. *Joginder Paul ke Shahkaar Afsane,* Book Channel, Lahore, 1996
13. *Bastian ,* Urdu Academy, Delhi, 2000
14. *Pachees,* Urdu Academy, Delhi, 2009

Collections of Flash Fiction (Micro stories)
1. *Silvaten ,* Lajpatrai & Sons, Delhi, 1975
2. *Katha Nagar,* Rabta Group, Delhi, 1986
3. *Parinday,* Taqheeqkar Publishers, Delhi, 2000
4. *Nahin Rehman Babu,* Educational Publishing House, Delhi, 2005

Novels and Novellas
1. *Aik Boond Lahoo Ki,* Maktaba-e-Afkar, Karachi, 1963 (Indian Edition, 1964)
2. *Amado Raft,* Indian Books Publications, Aurangabad, 1975
3. *Bayanat,* Indian Books Publications, Aurangabad, 1975
4. *Nadeed,* Rabta Group, Delhi, 1983
5. *Khwabro,* Educational Publishing House, Delhi, 1991 (Pakistan Edition, 1990)
6. *Paar Pare,* Insha Publications, Kolkata, 2004

Edited Volumes

1. *Naye Classic,* Marathwada University Aurangabad, 1973 (Urdu)
2. *New Urdu Fictions,* Katha, Delhi, 2004 (English)
3. *Asri Urdu Kahaniyan,* Penguin, Delhi, 2007 (Urdu)
4. *Naye Daur ki Urdu Kahaniyan,* Penguin, Delhi, 2008 (Hindi)

Criticism

1. *Rabta,* Taqhleeqkar Publishers, Delhi, 1997
2. *Be-Istelah,* Taqhleeqkar Publishers, Delhi, 1998

Select Translations of Short Stories and Novels by Joginder Paul Translations into Hindi

1. *Nadeed,* Rajkamal, Delhi, 1986
2. *Pratinidhi Kahaniyan,* Paperback, Rajkamal, Delhi, 1989
3. *Bayanat,* Saransh, Delhi, 1994.
4. *Kahan,* Collection of Short Stories, Kitabghar, Delhi, 1995
5. *Khwabro,* Rajkamal, New Delhi, 1996
6. *Charchit Kahanian of Joginder Paul,* Samayak, Delhi, 1997
7. *Parinday,* Vani Prakashan, Delhi, 2004
8. *Paar Pare,* Bhartiya Jnanpeeth, Delhi, 2004
9. *Nahin Rehman Babu,* Penguin India, 2005
10. *Ajanme,* Alekh Prakashan, Delhi, 2007
11. *Prem Sambandho ki Kahaniyan,* Naman Prakashan, Delhi, 2009
12. *Dharti ka Kaal,* Vani Prakashan, 2014

Translations into English

1. *The Story of India (Aamdo Raft* in Urdu), Kalamkar Prakashan, Delhi, 1981
2. *Sleepwalkers (Khwabro* in Urdu), Katha, New Delhi, 1999, 2001
3. *Selected Stories by Joginder Paul,* National Book Trust, New Delhi, 2004
4. *Black Waters,* (*Par Pare* in Urdu), Penguin India, 2007
5. *The Dying Sun,* Harper Collins Delhi, 2013
6. *Blind,* (*Nadeed* in Urdu), Harper Collins, Delhi, 2016

Some Translations into Other Languages

1. *Nadeed,* Mockba, Moscow, 1988 (Russian)
2. *Amad-o-Raft* (Punjabi)
3. *Selected Stories of Joginder Paul* (Kannada)
4. *Selected Stories of Joginder Paul* (Oriya)

Translators

Chandana Dutta has been assistant director for the publishing wing of Katha. She set up the publishing outfit Indialog of which she was chief editor. She was Editor, *Indian Horizons*, a quarterly on art and culture published by the ICCR, New Delhi. She translates from Hindi and Bangla into English. She holds a Ph.D from Jawaharlal Nehru University, New Delhi. She was adjunct faculty for the Masters Programme in Publishing at the Ambedkar University, Delhi, and is currently a member of the Advisory Committee for the Centre for Publishing there.

Keerti Ramachandra is a teacher by aptitude, inclination, and training, a translator by virtue of being multilingual and an editor as a result of long years of wielding the red pencil. She is an award-winning translator who translates fiction and non-fiction from Marathi, Kannada, and Hindi, and has edited for leading publishing houses. She is currently teaching an MA elective course in Translation Studies. She considers herself exceptionally lucky to be doing what she loves and to love what she is doing. After moving between four metros with her husband, she now lives in Bengaluru.

Meenakshi Bharat teaches in the University of Delhi and is a writer, translator and critic. Her special interests include children's literature, women's fiction, film studies, postcolonial literature and cultural studies – areas on which she has extensively researched and published. She has also published a book for children, *Little Elephant Throws a Party*, and has been crusading for children's literature studies. She has served as president of FILLM, and also as the treasurer of the Indian Association for the Study of Australia. (IASA).

Usha Nagpal is an MA in English from Delhi University and M.Litt in ELT (English Language Teaching) from Central Institute of English and Foreign Languages, Hyderabad, and also holds an M.Phil in Literary Linguistics from Strathclyde University, Glasgow. She retired as associate professor from Janki Devi Memorial College, Delhi University. A book of short stories by Joginder Paul, titled *The Dying Sun,* was co-translated by her and Keerti Ramachandra and published by Harper Collins.

Acknowledgements

To start with, we wish to express our thanks to Abu Zaheer Rabbani, Punya Prakash Tripathi and Chandana Dutta, each of whom has contributed to the idea of this book. Their input was significant in this trilingual translation project that involved Swahili, Urdu/Hindi and English. For Swahili words, thank you to the author's wife, Krishna Paul who helped us understand the words and their usage in Kenya.

The translators – Usha Nagpal, Keerti Ramachandra, Meenakshi Bharat – worked hard to capture the spirit of the original. We are grateful to have their impassioned labour bear fruit.

But of course…the book happened, thanks to Nirmal Kanti Bhattacharjee, Tultul De Niyogi and Trisha, our publishers. Shashi Bhushan patiently helped us prepare a clean manuscript after Vibha Kumar's in-house editing and our own editing of the text. Kudos to Misha's cover design that lent the book an appropriate aesthetic bearing.

Thank you all!

Sukrita Paul Kumar & Vandana R. Singh